Scientists have incomprehensible theories about parallel universes, ripples in time, relativity, and probability. Ordinary people think, while any of those theories is possible, strange events are just our own imagination messing with our heads, a reaction to drugs—legal or illegal—fate, or merely coincidence. *Of Unknown Origin* is a collection of stories based on actual incidents which defy explanation or, at the very least, logical explanations. They could be examples of any one of the above theories. Call them mysterious or a brush with the supernatural or just plain coincidence, these stories will give the reader something to think about or, at least, to be aware of the next time they encounter something of unknown origin.

KUDOS for *Of Unknown Origin*

In *Of Unknown Origins* by Trisha O'Keefe, we have fourteen short stories by this talented author. The stories are all completely different, except that they all deal with the paranormal or unexplained phenomenon. From a newlywed couple struggling to get by in the suburbs, to a mountaintop in Tibet, to the courtrooms of Greece, these clever tales will enlighten and entertain. O'Keefe has outdone herself to choose tales that are heartwarming, intriguing, and thought-provoking for a truly entertaining read. I loved it! ~ *Taylor Jones, The Review Team of Taylor Jones & Regan Murphy*

Of Unknown Origins by Trisha O'Keefe is a collection of short stories, fourteen in all, that all have something to do with the unexplained. From "The Man Who Wasn't There" and "The Battle of Taylor Springs," to "The House on the Hill" and "Mr. Angel," the author takes on a light-hearted, thought-provoking romp into the Unknown. Filled with delightful characters, vivid imagery, and interesting theories, *Of Unknown Origins* will keep you guessing and make you go, "Hummm..." Marvelous. ~ *Regan Murphy, The Review Team of Taylor Jones & Regan Murphy*

ACKNOWLEDGMENTS

I want to say thanks to Helen, who gave me the title for this book; Faith, my long-suffering editor; and all the staff at Black Opal. Thanks for putting up with me.

Of
Unknown
Origin

Trisha O'Keefe

A Black Opal Books Publication

GENRE: PARANORMAL/FANTASY

This is a work of fiction. Names, places, characters and incidents are either the product of the author's imagination or are used fictitiously, and any resemblance to any actual persons, living or dead, businesses, organizations, events or locales is entirely coincidental. All trademarks, service marks, registered trademarks, and registered service marks are the property of their respective owners and are used herein for identification purposes only. The publisher does not have any control over or assume any responsibility for author or third-party websites or their contents.

Of Unknown Origin

Chapter 1

THE MAN WHO CAME FROM NOWHERE

Melissa had only been married three months, much of which had been spent in motels until, at last, they found an apartment in half of an empty duplex. It was at the very edge of the small town, but the young couple didn't care. They had just moved out of graduate school housing, where you could practically hear the neighbors breathing through the cardboard walls. She and Bruce happily set up their barbeque pit in the backyard, which opened out on a farm field, and bought a picnic table at a yard sale to go with it. Melissa even started a little garden, to which Bruce had promised to add an addition that weekend. But he was called to corporate headquarters back east in New York, half a continent away.

She drove him to the airport, trying to look brave. It was the first time they had been apart since they were married. "It's like I'm being torn in half," she said, gulping the tears back.

"I wish we could afford two tickets, but we spent so long in motels, you know." His finger traced her lips. "Honey, I'll be back before you know it. Maybe even this weekend. Then I'll dig up that garden plot for the corn and stuff. I'll save up my per diem and get us some real nice steaks. And we'll have vodka collins, how's that?"

"Oh, no, you don't go shorting yourself just so you can buy expensive steaks. We'll have hot dogs and beer just like always. Just come home as soon as you can. I'll miss you so bad, it hurts already. Call me," she begged as he got out of the car.

"Promise," he said, blowing her a kiss.

Melissa cried all the way home, actually blubbering so long at one stoplight that a chorus of horns snapped her out of it. When she got home at the end of road, two little dogs ran out of the carport barking. Figuring they belonged to neighbors in the next block, she planned to give them a treat next time she saw them. She watched them tear up the road, wishing they had stayed around to make friends. Living in a motel was no place for an animal, but Bruce had promised her that, when they were settled, she could send for Bailey, her dog that she had left with her mom.

The crushing loneliness set in as soon as she opened the door and smelled the bacon she had fried that morning for Bruce. In order not to have a complete meltdown so early in the day, she turned on the TV and the CD player at the same time. Making herself a cup of coffee, she hurried upstairs without looking at the rumpled bed, changed into shorts, and put on an exercise video to complete the cacophony of noise.

That passed the morning. At noon, she called her mom who would be on her lunch hour back home. The familiar voice answered, "Hi, baby, how's it going?"

That was all it took. Melissa burst into tears. After a half-hour conversation spent reassuring her mother she hadn't married an axe murderer, she hung up, feeling mildly comforted. Social contact helped combat the awful loneliness, so Melissa decided to pay a visit to the small library in town. During the motel days, she had made friends with one of the younger librarians and, needing someone to talk to and something to read, she had found both in Sharon.

So the day passed, but when night fell and the town shut its doors, she finally had to go home. Melissa made herself an egg sandwich, took her book, an apple, and box of chocolate cookies and retreated to her bed. After a phone call from Bruce, she fell asleep with the light on.

In the middle of the night, the little dogs were back, raising hell outside her carport. She raised the bedroom window and told them to be quiet, figuring that would do it. It didn't, and it seemed nothing would. She put on her robe, went downstairs, and turned on the outside light which Bruce had told her to do, in spite of the electric bill.

"Hey, go home!" she shouted. "Shoo!"

The two scoundrels beat it up the road, but she remained there for a little longer, looking up at the wide canopy of stars. The dogs came back again and again, tearing up the road when she came out the front door. Finally, she fell asleep with cotton in her ears, a trick she had learned in the graduate school housing.

In the morning, she planned her schedule before she even got out of bed: put in a load of wash, exercise to the video, make herself a strawberry protein shake, hang the wash on the line in the back yard, wash the car—dirt seemed to cling to it—do something in the garden—watch the plants grow—and, in the afternoon, head back to the library.

Filled with determination, she put on her shorts and halter top, going through her routine like an athlete getting ready for a marathon. When the wash was done, she carried the basket out to the clothesline, thinking some poor stiff before her had the exactly same feeling that she had landed on a different planet.

He literally rose up from the weeds.

As she bent over to pull a wet sheet out of her basket and struggled to lift it by its corners, Melissa became aware there was a man standing at the edge of the pasture not ten feet from her, a tall, heavyset young man, and he was laughing. It was as if he were saying, "I've got you now and you can't do anything about it."

Her first urge was to scream, but a voice in her head stopped her. *Don't scream!* rang out loud and clear. As she straightened up to hang a piece of laundry, the man came barreling out of the weeds. In the same instant, Melissa lifted the heavy laundry basket and threw it directly in his path so that he stumbled over it.

Pivoting on one foot like a dancer, she took off running for the house, but he was advancing so fast with longer strides that she could hear him panting behind her. But she made it to the nearest door which she had left open, slammed it in his face, latching the screen just a split second before he grasped the handle.

There was a window beside it, and he ripped off the screen while she threw the deadbolt on the door and rushed to lock the window. That brought her face to face with her attacker and he had the same crazy grin, laughing at her ashen face. She went from window to window seeing if they were locked, with him just a second behind her. All he would have to do is get a rock and smash a pane of glass to reach the lock but he was looking for easier access. He disappeared for a split second and she thought he had gone for a rock. Then she thought about the front door! Had she thrown the deadbolt or had she left it unlocked in her sleep-deprived state last night?

Just then, her furry friends were back, barking furiously. She could only imagine them tearing at his trouser cuff, distracting him, giving her a chance to check the front door and throw the deadbolt.

She had left her cell phone upstairs in her bedroom, and she climbed the stairs two at a time, crashing into the room and there he was on the roof of the carport, almost at the window! Again, they met face to face as she locked the window before he reached it. The dogs went into frenzy below, and the man got a look of mad fury on his face. While he was distracted by the dogs, she found her cell phone under a pile of clothes and tried to dial nine-one-one, but she must have dialed Information instead because she got an automated voice recording. "What city and state, please?"

The man was at the window again, trying to raise it from the outside. She dialed nine-one-one again. And this time, a human answered, a woman with a twang like a banjo in her voice. "Nine-one-one, this is Roberta. How can I help you?"

"There's a man on the roof of my carport, trying to open a window. He chased me inside while I was hanging up my clothes in the backyard."

"Are you home alone, honey?"

"My husband's away. I think the man's got the lock broken—send somebody, quick! I'm going to make a run for it." She threw the phone down and ran downstairs out the front door. The man stopped tugging at the bedroom window and watched her tear up the street, the dogs following in her wake.

Melissa reached the first house and hammered on the front door. There was no one home. Then she looked down the road at her house. He was running up the road toward her, lumbering, out of breath, but still coming. She tried the next house and the next. They were empty! No car was parked in the garage or anywhere around, for the matter. She kept going, although the man was closing the gap between them, in spite of the racket the two little dogs made. When he was a few yards away, she could see he was laughing at her. It was obvious this was a bedroom community. There was no one home in the daytime. Just like Bruce, everyone worked in the city.

As luck, or something, would have it, not entirely everyone. A car turned down the dead end road, crawling along as though the driver was looking for an address, and Melissa frantically started waving it down.

"Hey! Hey! Help me, please!"

The car stopped and she began to sob with relief.

"Melissa? What on earth is the *matter*?" It was Sharon from the library. There was no time to explain. Melissa got in the backseat and locked the door. "I was just coming over to give the book you ordered," Sharon said, "and see if you wanted to go to the movies tonight."

The man had disappeared into the field again and the dogs stood in the road, their tongues lolling out, exhausted but alert for their next caper. The police had finally tracked the call to the small town, though it cost them precious minutes. Sharon stayed with her while the detectives crawled all over the house, coming to the conclusion that the stalker had spent the night on the roof outside her bedroom window.

"He'd have to know the town pretty well," one of them said, "or at least, the houses on this road to know there was no one home."

A local cop scoffed. "This ain't even a road. It used to be the fence line for that ranch over there until the damned developer built a few houses on it and called it whatever. Half of these places are empty, or gone into foreclosure." He came over to where the girls were standing. "You ought to have a big dog and a loaded gun to live out here, young lady." He was a burly man with iron-gray hair. "And you, young lady, ought you to be minding the store?"

Sharon had to stand on tiptoe to give him a hug. "Meet my father, Melissa. He's big on guns and dogs. Those two little bandits in the road are strays. Dumped by someone who moved out. Happens all the time. I tried to get them to come with me when I found them raiding the library dumpster. But they scoot right back here, to this duplex every time. So I guess you've inherited them, Melissa."

Two days later, they found the man lurking in the cemetery. He had escaped from a state facility for the criminally insane, Sharon said. Her father was the police chief and told her, in confidence, that the man had been arrested for raping and beating a woman nearly to death. But he was judged too insane to stand trial and committed for life. "That was three years ago," she said. "He has escaped twice during that time."

"Then this makes three times in three years. What do they have him in, a room with a revolving door?" Melissa was outraged, remembering his red, leering face when he thought she was defenseless.

"I guess he's like a Houdini or something. Don't worry, he won't be back. They're moving him to a different facility. One with maximum security."

No word ever appeared in the county newspaper or on the local TV news. When she asked Sharon why the news blackout, she only mumbled something about the state not wanting the newspapers to start an investigation of their institutions. "If you don't want to file charges, then that's the end of the matter as far as the police are concerned."

"What's the use? They'll only take him back to the funny farm."

When Bruce came home the following Monday, he found some changes had taken place in his absence. The tomato plants were filled with tiny green fruit, his wife had a part-time job at the local library, and two little dogs guarded the house, only letting him in the door because Melissa told them he could come in. In the following weeks, they put up a fence between the field and their backyard, they named the dogs Pete and Repeat, and Bruce bought Melissa a gun. It looked like a toy and she quickly put it away in a drawer so she wouldn't be reminded of what it was for.

The tomatoes ripened, Bruce went back to New York for a few days, saying if she wanted to stay with her mother, he understood. But Melissa liked her job at the library, she was making friends, and besides, who would take care of Pete and Repeat? No, Mama was out and the two marauders were in. Not that they stayed in. The call of the wild was too great and the pair of them would run off through the field chasing a rabbit or gopher. Or they would make the rounds on garbage pickup day, tipping over peoples' garbage cans on the curb.

One day, Melissa came home with her arms full of groceries and fished in her purse for the keys to the house. That was when she noticed the silence. The Jack Russell terrors weren't jumping all over her.

She let herself into the house, leaving the front door open while she put the groceries away, in case they showed up. Sticking her head out the door, she looked both ways up the road to make sure they weren't running or being chased by some irate neighbor. It wasn't garbage day so they must be out chasing the postman or a rabbit, she decided.

Melissa was busy putting her shopping when she heard a noise behind her. She turned and found the man standing behind her holding the limp body of Pete. He was laughing at her shock. "Dog's dead. Broken neck. He won't bark no more."

"Then we'd better bury him," Melissa replied calmly. "I'll show you where."

He thought it over then nodded. "Or he'll stink."

"Yes. That's what happens." Melissa opened the back door and walked into the back yard. She had left the shovel lying by the garden that morning where she was planting potatoes.

"That's what happens when you're dead," he repeated behind her.

She darted away from him, grabbed the shovel, and swung it, the full force of her anger behind the blow. The man's expression of surprise as the shovel hit him was imprinted on her memory forever. He went down like a felled tree. The limp body of Pete dropped from his inert hands. Melissa picked up the dog and cradled him. Even in death, he had managed to save her life.

On the ground, the man moved and groaned, blood spouting from his head. Melissa thought about finishing him with another blow. Then, still holding on to Pete, she went in the house and called the police. While she waited, she heard a whimper coming from the basement. It was Repeat tied up with a piece of string to a pipe.

A siren told her the police were here. She looked into the backyard. The man was gone, but not far. Repeat found him hiding behind a fir tree just beyond the little garden and barked until the police could march him away.

"You bad woman," he yelled at her as they led him away. "You hit me!"

"You killed my dog! If you ever come back here again, I'll do more than just hit you," Melissa yelled back. And marveled at her own strength.

Chapter 2

THE VIRGIN OF ZEITOUN

The year was 1978, about mid-April, when the apparition first appeared. People were going about their daily business, as usual, when a mechanic across the street from an ancient Coptic church in the old city looked up and saw a women walking across the roof. Thinking she was widow about to commit suicide, he called the police, but just as quickly as she appeared, she vanished.

I was a student at the American University in Cairo, Egypt, and determined to graduate the coming year, in spite of the precarious and unpredictable times. At the end of the Six-Day War, Israel had continued to make daily bombing runs on Helwan province, Egypt's industrial center. My mother was wiring frantic telegrams to the American Embassy, asking them to order all American students to leave. I ignored the rising tide of hysteria, having been sent back to the States the year before when hostilities reached the boiling point. Not about to have my studies interrupted a second time— whether they were holding Bar Mitzvahs at the Nile Hilton or not, as was the running joke, I was determined to graduate the following spring.

So when I heard that some kind of ghost was walking around on the roof of a Coptic church in the old section of the city, my reaction was "Oh, really?" and I immediately returned to my book, not in the least bit curious.

However, as the summer heat bore down like a hot iron on Cairo, the undercurrent of gossip reached a fever pitch even I couldn't avoid. It was everywhere—among the stately columns of the quad where the tables were filled with chattering students, at faculty cocktail parties, in the open market stalls of the city. What did the apparition mean? Was it predicting disaster? Drought? Plague? Israeli tanks rumbling through the narrow streets of the Mousskie?

I was still unmoved, even though no less a person than my hairdresser asked me if I had gone to see the Holy Virgin yet. That was the first time I'd heard the ghost referred to by name so I asked Achmed how he knew that it was Mary, the mother of Jesus.

As he was busy curling my hair, Achmed explained that, because the ghost was walking around the rooftop of the church built on the site of the olive tree where the family rested after fleeing from Jerusalem, word went around that it was the ghost of Mary hovering above the church.

"Why wasn't it Joseph or Jesus himself?" I asked.

Achmed did the Egyptian shrug. "I don't know. Maybe they were afraid of heights."

It was Mary and that was that. Women get all the jobs men don't want, I figured.

Before you think me too harshly critical, let me first give you some background on gossip in Egypt. First of all, Egyptians historically communicate verbally, face-to-face. That way they can judge the veracity of the person they are talking to and the quality of the conversation. After centuries of being lied to by a colonial government, everything else was put down as hogwash. Even the news you read in the papers was hogwash. If it was true, and you hadn't verified it with your own eyes, it was, at the very least, suspect. To that end, I had seen stories in the newspapers about grave robbers who plundered mausoleums in the City of the Dead and cut off the fingers of the corpses to get diamond rings, only to be haunted to the grave by the missing digit. One poor bloke tried to replace the missing finger sans the ring. He was found the next morning, lying in the looted grave atop the corpse he had desecrated—with his head bashed in.

During the aftermath of the Six-Day War, I was on my way to the bazaar, some ten miles away from my flat, when I witnessed one such published twisting of the truth. As usual, the air raid sirens went off about five minutes too late but we all knew to run for cover. When a truck full of soldiers pulled over, and the soldiers hunkered down in a ditch, I asked an officer what was wrong. He shrugged and pointed to the sky, which meant, in sign language, Israeli jets were coming. And seconds later, they did. Two Phantom jets, flying one on top of the other, streaked down the Nile toward Helwan, the industrial hub of Egypt.

The big guns opened up along the river and the show was on. It was over in a matter of seconds, though. The two jets, keeping under the radar, were gone in the blink of an eye. Then to the north, we saw a black column of smoke exploding in the clear morning sky.

People and soldiers cheered, thinking their obsolete anti-aircraft guns had downed an Israeli plane. But as I got closer to the city, I noticed a mob of people rushing toward what had to be the biggest garbage dump in the world. I asked a black-robed woman if she saw what color the downed plane was and a chorus answered me. "Iswid itayara!" they cried. A black plane, the color of Egypt's jets, not Israel's silver Phantoms and F-14s.

But the evening news blared that Egypt's mighty artillery had once again shot down an Israeli jet. I wondered what the pilot who landed in the garbage dump had to say about that revelation.

So to Achmed's inquiry that afternoon, I said that, even though I had been invited to go along with a group, I had no intention of going down into that part of Cairo at night or even in broad daylight to see a poor, distraught widow teetering on the brink of suicide, too afraid to jump and too afraid to live. I could see that he was itching to tell me something so I asked him if he himself had gone to see the phenomenon.

"I haven't been to see her yet because I'm afraid."

I could tell by his troubled expression that he was being truthful. I forgot to add the Muslims deified Jesus as one of their prophets along with Abraham, Mohammed being the chief one, however. "Could I ask why?"

"Well, they say you see her in proportion to the amount of good you have in you," he said earnestly. "My brother-in-law and sister went down there and she said, 'Oh, I see her face!'" He added, "My sister is a person who loves clothes and jewelry. You know, gold and such. Fancy clothes. Very vain. That is why she only saw the Virgin's face, not her whole self."

"Go on," I said, now fascinated.

"But my brother-in-law, he's a really bad man. He drinks whiskey, he smokes. Gambles on anything. When my sister said she saw the Virgin Mary's face, he said 'Where? Where? I don't a thing!'"

"So you think you won't see anything, is that it?"

He paused, a curling iron in mid-air. "I think not, unless you come with me. Having a date with a Christian girl might do the trick."

I hated to spoil his backup plan, but I ducked that invitation, too, saying I was just too busy studying for finals. "But if she comes out here, then I'll go see her," I said, jokingly referring to the suburb of Cairo where I and the rest of ex-pat lived.

But I think he got the point. I didn't believe the hype around what I thought was just a publicity stunt to attract tourists in hard times.

As Christmas approached, the long hours of cramming got to me, and I caught one of Egypt's mysterious fevers. To the point, when my roommate left for a Christmas Eve party I had bought a new dress especially for, I was just too sick to go. I took to my bed, feeling sorry for myself and imagining what was going on in my absence. As the clock struck eleven, the fever took over. I fell asleep, dreaming of all the dazzling men I would have met if I had been at the blasted party.

The hall clock struck twelve. Without opening my eyes, my first sensation was of a presence very near me, so near I could almost feel breath on my face. I kept my eyes closed, a short parade of possibilities going through my mind. Very short, in fact. It was either my roommate

Cynthia, come to check on me and gloat. The other possibility was a burglar had climbed in the window and was checking to see if I would scream. I didn't want to speak to either so I kept playing possum, hoping both would go away.

Then I opened my eyes. Hovering above me, her great glowing Byzantine eyes inquiring into mine, black hair streaming out, arms outstretched as though she was flying, was what I can only describe as a vision. Call it something my feverish mind had dreamed up, call it a ghost of heaven, call it whatever passed for description in the limited human language. I had since called it—only to myself—The Lady of Stars because that is the way I remembered her.

She was dressed in a long blue dress that was totally made of stars, trailing off like a comet's tail into a brilliant train of light. But her eyes were thoroughly human, brimming with compassion, prying beyond my closed eyelids, seeing through my calloused nature into my very heart. That was, if the soul hid there. When I opened my eyes and saw her, I suddenly had the feeling I had caught her out, checking on me the way my mother would if she were there. It was as if she was afraid of being revealed as the ultimate helicopter mom.

I was so shocked, I squeezed my eyes shut, took a deep breath, and then opened them again. She was gone and, in the next millisecond, I willed her to come back. But she didn't. I sat bolt upright and saw that the clock beside my bed was still pointing at midnight. The chair at the foot of my bed, over which I had carelessly thrown my robe, was exactly where it was when I saw The Lady of Stars. Everything in the room was exactly the same, except I was covered with sweat. My fever had broken, and I was feeling hungry again. I was going to be all right. Back in California, on her way to work on the 405, my mom relaxed.

Chapter 3

THE BATTLE OF TAYLOR SPRINGS

I saw it from the scratchy backseat of my uncle Quentin's Mercury Cougar one afternoon when we were taking a Sunday drive.

I sat beside my sister who was alternating between reading *The Great Gatsby* and being carsick. Then we passed two vine-covered wrought iron gates with what had been a circular drive. There was a huge hulk of a house lurking behind an Italianate fountain, although the Georgia jungle had long ago obscured it from view. However, something about the whole scene seemed to beckon for help like a drowning victim going down for a third time.

"Stop!" I said, interrupting a droning conversation about football between the two men in the front seat.

"You're being rude, baby," my father said without turning. "If your sister is going to be sick again, roll down the window."

"I'm not," my sister said to *The Great Gatsby*. "Be quiet, brat."

"But I saw a big house back there. It had a real fountain with water and birds."

"So what?"

"That's Bon Sejour," my uncle Quentin said. He was always the official tour guide because he worked for the county tax commissioner's office and knew everything about property taxes. "It's an old place. Falling apart."

The two men in front launched into tales they knew of people who had lost their shirts—I pictured running around half naked—trying to restore these old places. My uncle said he knew of one man who committed suicide and the conversation went on from there.

My last glimpse of Bon Sejour was from the back window of the scratchy Mercury Cougar. The chimneys of the house were barely visible through the tangle of jungle vines enveloping the trees, but they seemed to call out to me, like people being swept out to sea on a river of kudzu.

Twenty years later, I went in search of it again. I had no idea why I wanted to see it, I just did. Maybe because my request to stop was dismissed so long ago, maybe in search of the unknown. Anyway, there I was on the same stretch of road, surrounded by the verdant green sea.

I passed nothing but hunting cabins, doublewides, and fishing camps. Finally, I pulled into a one-pump gas station and bait store. I bought some chips and a can of soda to reassure the rustic types sitting around in wooden rocking chairs I wasn't a narcotics agent looking for meth labs. "Would you all know of a place with a French name around here?"

That set off a ripple of hoots from the locals. Finally, they sobered up. "There used to be a place called something like seizure up the road." one said, "but it's been a fishing camp for a while now."

"You talking about that the old place on Taylor Lake, miss? My grandma used to call that place the Lachlan house, said it was the finest place around for miles."

One old geezer with a scraggly beard dipped snuff, spilling a few crumbs on his hairy chin. "Looks more like east hell to me."

A man in faded overalls stood up. "Here, I'm going that way. If you'll follow me, I'll show you where it's at."

I followed him back the way I'd come. The reason why I missed it was now clear. The wrought iron gates were gone, and the fountain I had seen from the road as a kid was gone, too. The front of the house was almost obscured by a rusting school bus parked across the entrance. The only thing I recognized was the second floor gallery which had blankets hung over the railings. The roof was a patchwork of plywood, metal, and wood shingles, but the windows were still held their French lines, although they were boarded up with graffitied plywood now.

I parked in front and tried to get in the yard, but a pit bull stopped me, emerging like a fast freight from under one of the many rusting truck carcasses.

"She won't bite, ma'am."

But not wanting to be the first victim of mistaken confidence, I got back in my car, waiting until the man had called the dog back.

"What can I do for you, ma'am?" He was as seedy as the yard, grizzled, dirty hair sticking from under his John Deere cap.

Not knowing exactly what I was doing there, I lied. I had noticed a hand-lettered sign as I drove in the yard so I told him I was looking for a good place to bring my son, who wanted to learn to fish.

That apparently struck home. "Ma'am, you've come to the best place around for that. Stocked with bass and grouper, cat, open year round."

As we strolled around to the lake—if strolling was the right word for picking the way around truck tires and rusting guts of cars, with a heavy breathing pit bull hoping for a misstep—I asked my guide about the house.

"Been empty almost eighty years now. When the last family moved out, nobody wanted it, so I kind of took it over." Which meant he was squatting. "See that trailer across the lake." I squinted through the mist settling on the grayish water. "That's home," he said. "That's where I live now."

I noticed a small fenced area with a few impressive monuments rising above the tall weeds. The centerpiece was a small mausoleum topped with draped urns fashionable in Victorian cemeteries. The name of the family was carved on the lintel. It was McDowell. I felt the wet nose of the dog on my bare leg as I stopped short. "That name. It's somewhere in my family tree, I think."

"Could be. Everybody who's lived around here any time is related, one way or another. Want to see the lake up close?" my guide said, ignoring the dog.

"Could I do that later? I have to get back." I couldn't wait to leave and start digging in the family dirt for the McDowell connection. Surprisingly, it was easy to find. A great-great-great aunt had married a Major Lachlan McDowell from South Carolina. He had been killed in the Revolutionary War when the Carolina and Georgia militias encountered the Royal Scottish Highlanders in a pitched battle at Taylor Springs. Most of the militia men were wiped out, but Major McDowell had an heir, Douglas McDowell, and so the line staggered on until after the Civil War. With WWI, it was petering out. No mention of Bon Sejour.

In an old topographic map, I found a Taylor Springs within the land holdings of one Stuart McDowell, circa. 1926. It coincided exactly with the spot where the lake was behind the house. I dragged my fifteen-year-old Max, kicking and spitting, over to the fishing camp.

"But, Mom, I hate fishing! It's so boring! Give me a break, will you?"

But his pitiful protests fell on deaf ears. "Men have died who were not much older than you so you could be bored, so be bored," I said.

"What is with you all of a sudden? You've gotten hyped on this history crap because you're writing a story for some magazine nobody ever reads."

"Watch your language!"

"Sorry, Mom, but I just don't get it." He stopped, goggled-eyed, as we arrived at the fishing camp that was Bon Sejour. "Holy crap!" He looked awed by the sight of so much dereliction.

I had a moment's peace, in which I said, "Pretend you want to fish."

He just nodded.

I had done research on the Battle of Taylor's Springs, which I found, thanks to my uncle Quentin, now retired, in the journals of the Georgia Militia circ 1775. While the resident squatter, whose name was Jamie, was man-splaining with Max about fishing bait or something, I walked the path around the lake with the pit bull Reba at my heels. I didn't know what I hoped to find but, as I walked, the strangest feeling came over me, an overwhelming kind of sadness, almost depression. I couldn't, for the life of me, figure out why. I had contrived to get here, and I ought to be overjoyed at being able to explore.

I was an historian—hardly a revelation, given my interest in old places. I taught American History at a local state university when they had the funding. Otherwise, I wrote for history journals about the places I'd researched and hoped I get published. So I was used to "creepy places," as Max invariably called them.

But this place slowly closed its grip on me as I found myself on the bend of the lake, far from where Max was putting his pole into the water. Reba started to growl, a bad sign at best. I looked around and she was staring fixedly at the weeds around the banks of the lake. I stopped in my tracks and then, out of the weeds, a rattlesnake came sluggishly across the path a few feet ahead. Though I had made sure to wear my thick hiking boots, I stood there, my blood frozen, in spite of the heat, as it made its way to the weeds on the other side and disappeared. We heard its warning rattle across the field.

"That was close. Thank you, Reba." I leaned down to pet her and, surprisingly, she turned into a lap dog. Waving her narrow rear around, she snuggled up against my leg like my cat at home, her weight nearly bowling me over. "Way to go."

As I bent down, a gleam of metal in the weeds by the lake caught my eye. Risking another snake encounter, or even an alligator lurking in the weeds, I cautiously made my way down the embankment and, with my knife, pried a metal shotgun cartridge out of the moist earth. Someone, possibly Jamie, had been duck hunting.

As I got to the other side of the lake, a mist started settling on the woods beyond, creeping toward the water. It was the last week of May so darkness wouldn't come for another three hours yet, but I knew that springs, especially in coastal Georgia, had climates all their own. A chill came with the mist, contrasting sharply with the heat of the sun. With Reba now patrolling ahead of me, I decided to go on, when I heard Jamie shouting something, Thinking Max had caught something besides an old tire, I continued on around the lake. Every once in a while, Reba would stop and stare at the woods as if she saw another menace, until she finally stopped for good, not willing to go any farther. Lowering her head, she emitted a low, deep growl that rumbled in her throat.

Then giving me one inscrutable look, she turned back as if to say, "Go no farther. If you do, you'll go without me. I'm out of here."

I stood for a while peering into the woods, looking for whatever she saw that made even a bear-fighting dog decide that discretion was the better part of battle. My imagination got the better of me, thinking of what might be in there, and I followed Reba back to reality.

That was the first of many trips to the lake that summer, ostensibly to take Max and his friends fishing, with Jamie welcoming the increase in business. With Reba as my guide and bodyguard, I roamed the grounds at will. "But I wouldn't get far off the road if you're afraid of snakes," Jamie warned.

"Don't worry. Reba won't let me," I assured him.

One day in the fall, I plunged off the road into the woods with Reba soon taking the lead. For some time, she disappeared into the ferns that were everywhere on the forest floor, a sort of sub-forest. When I caught up with her, I saw she was standing by a hole, peering inside. As I looked around I saw that wasn't the only hole—in fact, the whole place looked like a battle field, pitted with foxholes. Someone had been digging all around the place, not even bothering to fill in the holes. I remembered the only time I discussed the possibility that the manmade lake covered what remained of the Battle of Taylor Springs with Jamie.

"The Revolutionary War? I thought we were against the Yankees in that one."

Patiently, I filled in the gaps in American history, at which he was amazed.

"You mean that sword I—my friend—found down there was a hundred years older than 1860?"

He described the sword he had found as inscribed along the blade and handle with engravings. When I asked if I could see the sword, Jamie had the grace to look guilty. "Sorry, he already sold it online. I guess he needed the money."

"I guess," I said. "How much did he get for it, do you know?"

He told me for fifty bucks his friend had sold the sword of Birmingham steel engraved with what had likely been a family motto as well as the name of the officer it belonged to.

"Do you think it was worth more?"

I couldn't even answer him, knowing what it had meant to the family that was grieving for their son, whether British or Patriot. As an historian, I wanted to lecture him on the theft of artifacts, but looking around at where and how he lived, I reminded myself that what was one century's glory was another's dust.

Now, Reba began digging in the hole in front of her as if she had spotted as animal. As red dirt flew between her legs, she grasped something in her powerful jaws and pulled it out of the soil.

"What did you find, girl?" I asked.

As if she were proud to present me with a token of her affection, she dropped a black stick at my feet. I was just about to pitch it for her when something white caught my eye down in the hole. There were more blackened sticks, some showing white in sharp contrast with the black soil. I looked again at the thing in my hand. It wasn't a stick. It was a human bone, probably a rib bone. These were human remains.

In my horror, I dropped it and Reba, thinking I was playing a game, snatched it up and ran off. The Battle of Taylor Springs replayed in my mind now in all its gory detail. The patriots were outnumbered by the British troops, almost three to one, and facing the Royal Scottish Highlanders, known as the fiercest of soldiers, willing to fight to the death. They were further reinforced by two "grasshopper" cannons.

On the patriot side were sixty Georgians, forty South Carolina militiamen, two French officers, some Creek Indians, and a handful of volunteers. It was a rout. The British lost three men, seventeen wounded. Sixty of the patriots were killed, the wounded dragging the dying to the shelter of the corn fields, fearing what would happen if the British took them prisoner. The British then set fire to the corn field, ignoring agonized cries of the wounded men who were trapped there.

"Told you there was stuff down here," said a voice behind me. "Bet that was what you were after all the time, wasn't it?"

It was Jamie and he was holding his shotgun.

"You've been digging around down here, selling stuff off online, haven't you? Did you know there were bodies not three feet under the dirt down here? That's grave-robbing, Jamie. You do know that's a federal offense, don't you?"

"I have a right to sell any stuff I find. I live here, don't forget." There was a note of uncertainty in his voice.

"You and I both know you're a squatter, Jamie." I kept my eye on his gun. We were both on uncertain ground, because this was private land and not on the Historic Register while he had squatter's rights with no one around who could evict him. "Besides you've got to have some respect for the brave men who died here."

"They're dead, that's the difference. I'm alive and I have to eat to stay that way, you know." He took a couple of steps forward and raised his shotgun. Reba came back and took up a position by my legs, as though protecting me. "Reba, you come here right now, you damn mutt! You hear me? Now!"

Reba didn't budge but leaned harder against my legs. I could feel her powerful body trembling.

"Damn dog! I said come—"

What happened next came in rapid sequence. Jamie took another step forward, his foot went down into the hole Reba had dug. He went down with a curse, the gun went off harmlessly, raining buckshot at the trees. "My leg's broke!" he screamed. "Help me! Do something!"

Reba went over to him, cautiously, to see if it was safe. I took the opportunity that had been handed to me, God only knew how, and ran for my life. Once in the car, I called nine-one-one, took one last look at Bon Sejour, and headed for home. I never went back, but I did call the

Historic Register and report my find. And, of course, I wrote an article on the Battle of Taylor Springs. While revisiting the journals of the Georgia Militia to get my facts straight, I noticed a strange notation. One of the Georgians had a bear-hunting dog whose name was Tiberius. During the battle, during the hand-to-hand combat, Tiberius threw himself between his master and a British bayonet, saving his master's life but losing his own. During the retreat, his master had to leave the body of his dog behind and regretted it deeply.

Chapter 4

DEEP WOODS

We Southern women are tough as nails on the outside but marshmallows within. Therefore, it follows the males should be square-jawed versions of Clint Eastwood—gun-toting, spitting accurately, and cussing a blue streak.

This describes my male cousins, which is why this story is all the more believable.

When two of my cousins took it in their heads to go hunting one night down in a swamp where I wouldn't even set foot in the daytime, no one thought they were crazy. Nobody but me. Not even if someone told me there was buried treasure three feet inside the treeline, would I go there. I told them so.

This swamp is the site of an old Mississippian burial mound and rumor has it, some funny things have happened there. Funny enough so that people just pack up and get the hell out, too scared to talk about what they've seen.

That was the gossip among the old timers that sat around in the squeaky rocking chairs on the front porch of the gun and bait shop at the edge of the vast tangle of vines, live oaks with arms ready to behead the unwary, and pools that held things you didn't know existed.

"Out for some hunting before the warden starts his rounds?" asked an old-timer as Robbie and Len came up the steps.

The cousins said they were and another gaffer asked, "Been here before?"

They said they had. The front porch jury consulted among themselves.

The foreman spoke. "Well then, you know what goes on here at night. Lots of drug dealers around here. Meth labs pop up all the time."

"You trying to scare us off which stories about the Chinaberry Man? Sir, I heard that story all my life and never seen hide nor hair of him," answered Robbie with the swagger of one seasoned by danger. "Wish I could."

A man who they assumed was the store owner because he had an apron on that said Night- rawlers and

Worms came out to join the conversation. "A while back, we had two men from out of state. Think they were TV people or some such mess. Anyway, they had a couple of dogs with 'em and camped down by the creek. Up and left in the middle of the night, they did. Left a lot of their gear, too. Tent, sleeping bags, and missing one of the dogs."

That was greeted with grunts of disapproval. Nobody leaves a dog in the swamp for gators to eat.

"What do you expect from them TV people?"

"How do you know they were missing a dog if they left in the middle of the night?" Len asked. He was studying the law and prosecution was his thing.

"'Cause they stopped for breakfast at the diner and told ol' Joey they did."

"They say why they bailed out in such a hurry?"

"No, but he noticed their hands were shaking so much, they couldn't hold the coffee without spilling it all over the place."

Everybody chuckled at that and got another handful of boiled peanuts out of the warmer.

Undeterred by stories, the cousins left their truck at the trailhead and hiked to the first deer stand, about a quarter of a mile into the woods. They had miners' lights on their hunting caps, their knapsacks held sleeping bags and beer. They both carried their rifles, in case of snakes or meth dealers.

The bolder of the two, I'll call him Robbie, went on to the second deer stand about a mile and a half farther into the swamp. He told Len, the less experienced hunter, to stay where he was and, if there was any trouble, fire two shots in the air. They agreed to meet in the morning back at the truck.

Robbie continued on, deeper into the swamp, well-fortified by Jack Daniels. At some point, a branch cracked behind him and, thinking it was a deer, he turned around. Taking his flashlight from his belt, he scanned the woods behind him. Seeing nothing, he continued on, concentrating on negotiating the forest floor. He had been here in daylight enough to know there was a stream up somewhere ahead and alligators on its banks. They didn't snap at humans unless one stepped on it, but he was careful not to risk a misstep.

Then he heard it again—a snapping twig, a crunching of underbrush. He stopped and whatever was making the noise halted somewhere in the thicket behind him. Robbie took a few more steps and hesitated. Whatever it was stopped too, but not without taking another step.

By this time, Robbie figured whatever it was following him was about parallel with him but shielded by the massive foliage.

"Len, where are you, man? I'm over here, you idiot!" Just like Len not to follow his directions, Robbie thought. Probably got scared staying by himself. Only the throbbing of the frogs and cicadas answered him. "Len, that you?" He shone his light through the bushes. That's when he smelled the peculiar odor of chinaberries. Robbie felt the hair on his head stir at the roots. The back of his neck prickled like it had in Iraq when a sniper was nearby.

He knew one thing. That wasn't a deer over there or anything walking on four legs. Whatever it was walked upright. Robbie took the safety lock off his gun and, treading as quietly as he could, moved on down the trail at a brisk pace. He wasn't far from the deer stand now, only a few hundred yards.

That's when both his lights went out— simultaneously. That shook him up. He had put new batteries in both the flashlight and the miner's light before he left home.

Shoving his flashlight in his belt and holding his rifle chest-high in case he tripped over a root or fell in a hole, Robbie began to jog. He was sweating now, not from the heat—it was a cool night—but from fear. Fear had its own distinct smell.

The footsteps increased their pace, too, not behind him, but parallel with him through the thicket.

Following the trail by moonlight wasn't easy, but fear heightens all the senses. Now as he neared the deer stand, he figured the creek was still about thirty feet away. He and his hunting buddies had built the stand with that in mind, knowing the deer drank there at night. In

Robbie's mind, he could see the creek that ran by the
burial mound curve inland upstream from the stand.
Whatever was following him would have to cross it
before he did. Holding his breath, silencing his own
breathing, he heard a splash as if something heavy had
plunged into the water.

As he reached the safety of the stand and climbed up,
he heard his stalker wading through the creek, heading
upstream. It was taking steps, not as an animal moves
through water, but in strides as a man on two legs would
do. By the light of the full moon, he saw a familiar
oblong shape rising just above the trees across the water.
For the first time, he realized he was standing directly
across the creek from the old burial mound.

Then, as the footsteps faded, both his flashlight and
the miner's light came back on. Robbie fumbled for the
army-issue canteen on his belt and took a couple of
swallows of Jack Daniels.

In the morning, the two hunters rendezvoused at the
truck. "You see any deer?" Robbie asked, still thinking
Len had played a trick on him.

Len yawned and stretched. "Hell, no. Gave up after
you left and went back to the truck to sleep. Damned
mosquitoes were killing me out there."

When Robbie told me this story, I avoided the
temptation to say I told you so. I assumed he'd learned
his lesson, since it had been two years since he'd been
hunting in the swamp. For whatever reason, he had stuck

to the rented tract of woods and the comfort of his ATV since that night at the mound.

But the call of the two deer stands he and Len had built was too hard to resist. When hunting season opened the next fall, he decided to go where he knew the deer drank at night—the creek that ran by the ancient burial mound. This time he took an experienced hunting buddy along, just to make sure his old nemesis PTSD wasn't kicking up. Len had declined to go this time, citing the Georgia Bar Exam coming up.

Again, Robbie and his baddy stopped at the old bait store about half a mile from the swamp to buy some more ammo and beer. The usual old timers were there, swapping stories and complaints. The conversation stopped when the two strangers walked in. They exchanged the proper greetings with the old timers, followed by the usual talk about the weather.

"Where you'all from?"

"Westville." That got a few nods. Local boys, not from out of state or tourists.

"Ever hunted here before?"

Robbie said he had, many times. His buddy shook his head.

The good old boys' attention was then focused on Robbie. "Ever seen or heard anything out of the ordinary?"

Robbie hesitated. "Depends on what you mean by out of the ordinary. A couple skinny dipping, drunk as skunks. A meth lab in an old truck. Lots of drinking parties."

The old farmers looked at each other and back at Robbie. One spat expertly in a coffee can in the corner. "Well, be careful after nightfall, son. And keep that rifle handy. Never can tell what you might run into. "

When they got back in the truck, his buddy asked him, "What was that about? They acted like we were going into combat."

Robbie just shrugged, snapped the pop-top from his beer can, and took a long drink. "Just curious old farts. Makes a change from the weather, I guess."

This time the two of them went down to the deer stand on the creek. Making a fire, they fried burgers and fries on their camp stove and drank a six pack. "I'll take the first watch," said his friend. "I'll wake you up if anything shows up worth shooting."

Robbie climbed up to the platform and promptly fell asleep, thanks to the throbbing cicadas and the beer. He awoke with a start, wide awake. Something was wrong. He was alone in the deer stand.

He sat up and looked around for his friend. Probably gone to take a leak he thought. By the position of the moon, he could tell it was early hours of the morning. Down below, the fire had burned down to coals. Across the creek, the old burial mound seemed to glower at him through a funky mist rising from its base. A light breeze shifted the mist around as if the ghosts of the natives buried there were dancing as they had done in the long distant past.

A footstep in the forest nearby caused Robbie to freeze. He grabbed for his rifle and waited as if he had been cast in stone. Another footstep followed the first. A deer, Robbie told himself or his friend returning to camp. But something in the back of his mind said it wasn't either of those options.

He tried to yell at his friend but his voice wouldn't obey him. Just then a large shadow fell across the clearing below him. Robbie clutched his rifle harder but his head refused to lower so he could look through the telescopic site. He could feel the hair on the back of his neck rising, the way it had done the last time he was here. All he could do was wait.

As if it could smell his fear, the shadow lingered at the edge of the light from the coals for a few seconds. Then it disappeared, and Robbie heard whatever it was walking away through the woods. It left behind the faint odor of chinaberries.

Presently, his friend returned, carrying his rifle and a roll of toilet paper. Robbie relaxed again, hearing the purposeful stride of a man.

His friend put the toilet paper away and climbed up beside Robbie. "Sorry, I had to take a dump. Say, you didn't come looking for me, did you?"

"No, why?"

His friend shook his head. "Nothing. I just thought I heard something. Must have been a deer rustling around. Damn things always show up when you're not ready. Go back to sleep. I'm wide awake, anyway. Might as well pull an all-nighter."

"I'll keep you company."

The two hunters lay side by side in the deer stand, watching the clearing below them, but not for deer.

Chapter 5

THE ROYAL GRIFFIN INN

According to the guidebook, The Royal Griffin had been in continuous service for 800 years—give or take a few years out for wars, plagues, and natural disasters.

"From the looks of the place," commented my friend, Charles, looking up at the wainscoted exterior, "it just barely survived all of the above. Just take a look at that crossbeam," he said, his architect's hand sweeping along the central beam which had a distinct downward curve. "I hope the floors don't look like that."

They did. In fact, the whole place seemed to be teetering on the edge of collapsing into the quaint Welch

village whose name looked like alphabet soup. The desk
clerk, too, was appropriately ancient, looking down his
long Welch nose at our sweatshirts and jeans. "Will that
be two rooms or one, sir?"

"We don't have to stay here," I whispered. "Let's
just get a drink in the bar and keep going until we get
cross the border. There's bound to be something decent in
England. And less creepy."

"Mommy, I feel like I'm going to throw up again,"
groaned my five-year-old son, Jeremy.

"Have you got a suite, possibly?" I could tell my
boyfriend Charles didn't want a shirt full of Jeremy's
vomit again. Once a day was enough for that kind of
surprise He was already distancing himself by stepping
up to the desk and signing the register.

"The water closet is to your left, madam." The desk
clerk appeared to be preparing for another catastrophe
behind the battlements of his huge reservations desk. He
whipped out a plastic baggie and disposable wipes.
"Here," he said, thrusting them at me. "Just in case the
tyke doesn't make it to the WC."

After a couple of stiff ones in the bar, we decided to
investigate our rooms. With the resiliency of five-year-
olds, Jeremy was recovering, leading the way down the
long wavy halls. "It's like the fun house," he called over
his shoulder.

The pompous desk clerk who insisted on showing us to our rooms, sniffed through his long nose. "As with all very old buildings, sir," he said.

"He's right, you know. I'd surely hate to navigate these halls after a night of heavy drinking," said Charles. "I'll wager you have some people wandering around who've never made it to their rooms."

His public school voice made it clear you could dress a man in sweatshirt and jeans but you couldn't disguise an upper class accent. Nor could I disguise my American one and didn't bother trying.

Our guide sniffed again, as though he didn't approve of such transcontinental relationships. "Over the years, we have collected quite a few lost...er...guests, yes, sir. Right this way," the clerk said, opening a massive door. The room could have housed giants. Everything was oversized—the Henry VIII curtained bed, armoire, and a massive desk with Griffin feet.

Even Charles was impressed in his upper-class way, I could tell. But all he said was, "Is there a maid who will come stay with the child while we have dinner?"

"Of course, sir," the clerk sniffed, regarding the child as if he were an insect in a collection.

"Look, Mommy! There's even a ladder for me to climb up on the bed." Before I could stop him, Jeremy tore free of my hand and ran to the bed, where he promptly threw up on the brocade coverlet. No plastic baggie or wet wipe for him. He had to have a whole bedspread. He looked around at our horrified faces. "Sorry."

"At least it wasn't on me this time," said my gallant knight.

After an awkward dinner, during which Charles drank more than he ate, we made our way down the labyrinthine hall to our room. Charles hesitated outside the door. "We navigated rather well without our GPS, didn't we, darling?" A few brandies had made him horny again and he gave me a wet kiss tasting of booze. "Let's hope the little fellow is fast asleep.

The little fellow turned out to be out cold in the adjoining room, and, after the maid tiptoed out, Charles followed suit without even taking off his shoes. Traveling with American ex-pats had proved to be more than he could handle. I made him as comfortable as I could and then climbed up on the other side of the Henry the VIII bed, visualizing some fine lady vaulting up beside her lord in her long nighty.

As I lay there, reading the guidebook, the room seemed to take on a life of its own, making strange groans and sighs, the way very old things did. Aside from being made for Cyclops and his brothers, I decided there was something strange about this room. The high ceiling was lost from view in the shadows cast by the converted gas lamps, and there was a cold breeze coming from somewhere, despite the thick, ornate drapes at the towering windows and around the bed. Maybe it was coming from the magnificent fireplace, I thought, hoping that was all that would come across the massive hearth yawning like a Cyclops's mouth, its great, black teeth yearning to take a bite of soft flesh. At the very least, visions of legions of mice running across the floor to leap up on the bed made me cuddle even closer to Charles, but he just rolled over on his side presenting me with his back. I was on my own, my lord said in effect.

Charles and I had met in London where he was guest speaker at a seminar on the preservation of historic buildings, which I had to take as part of my job as a city planner. Being a prominent architect specializing in historic preservation, he made a perfect guide around the city, especially the pubs and, eventually, the trendy night life in Soho. There wasn't much future in this romantic interlude—I was a single parent with a child, he had a pedigree a mile long and an ex-something with a baby. But when I said I wanted to tour the Welch lake country, he offered to be our guide and show us around in his Porsche. What I could say but yes?

As the replica of Big Ben in the corner struck eleven and a clock tower somewhere in the village echoed each stroke, I tried to concentrate on the guidebook, wanting badly to make a success out of this tour of the Welch lake country. The castle the clerk had mentioned was built around the time of the Norman invasion, presumably by one of King Arthur's buddies. It had been inhabited by the same family up until the 1700s, when they backed the wrong side in a fight. It was now a bed and breakfast, presumably under new management.

I must have fallen asleep at that point, because when I awoke, the room was totally dark except for light filtering from the street through the drapes. I knew I had fallen asleep with the lights or at least I hadn't turned them off. Blackouts were commonplace in old places with wiring from back in Edison's time, I reasoned, but if Jeremy awoke and his Tigger nightlight had gone out—

A strange sound sent an electric shock shooting right through me. The hair on the back of my neck began to stir. I was simply frozen rigid with fear, afraid to move or speak, but listening for what had sent me into this state of paralysis. Then it came again—slow, heavy footsteps in the corridor approaching our door, but without the squeaking that usually accompanied anyone walking down the hall. When they stopped, I slid my eyes in that direction and saw the brass door handle turning slowly, up and down, catching the light as it moved. The village clock was chiming twelve, but Big Ben was silent. Then the ponderous footsteps moved slowly down the hall.

It took me a full five minutes to recover my wits enough to rationalize that somebody had just gotten the wrong room, when I realized that someone was standing just to the left of the fireplace. A figure in white! Unreasoning fear took over again, and I squeezed my eyes shut. When I opened them again, the figure had vanished. In what seemed like ages, my heart started beating again.

Jeremy! I leaped out of bed, what seemed to be two floors down, and tiptoed to the adjoining door. He was sound asleep, sucking his thumb. I seemed to be the only one awake in the whole world, except the happy wanderer in the hall.

I climbed back up beside Charles again, wishing I could wake him up. But he would only chuckle indulgently and say, "Didn't I tell you? Probably some poor sod lost their GPS."

I decided not to be the Ugly American, complaining about no ice in the drinks and no toilet paper in the loos. I had just dozed off when it happened again. The village clock struck one, the footsteps in the hall, the door handle turning, and the ghostly figure in the long white dress appearing and disappearing by the fireplace. Repeat performance at two, then, at three o'clock, something else happened. The shimmering figure in white began to move straight toward the bed. I squeezed my eyes shut and opened them to find a woman's face, mouth gaping, her eyes rolled upward with a look of fear and horror I couldn't even describe. I opened my mouth to scream, but no sound came out. Then the figure in white retreated, moving toward Jeremy's room. My eyes slid to follow her as she glided past the bed.

But something was different about the form, some alteration. As she passed the window, the light from the street lamp passed through her gown, and then I saw that the woman's head was missing. Then blending with the filmy curtains, she disappeared into the night.

In the next instant, the lights came back on. When I was sure I wouldn't drop dead the minute I hit the floor, I jumped down and peeked into Jeremy's room. He was sleeping soundly, cradling his scrap of blankie. As I returned to bed, I noticed Big Ben started ticking again. It was only twelve-thirty. I checked my cell phone to make sure. I must have dreamed the whole thing!

The next morning, Charles awoke refreshed and hungry. "How did you sleep, princess?"

An involuntary shiver passed through me, although he often called me his American princess because I was so picky about everything. "Just fine, except for the traveling salesman who kept getting our room mixed up with his."

I told him the whole story over breakfast, leaving out the part about the headless woman in case he would think I was on drugs. The dining room was virtually empty so Charles called the headwaiter over to ask if there were any other guests on our floor.

The waiter did a good job of looking puzzled, I thought. "No, sir. May I ask why you're inquiring?"

"No particular reason, except my wife here kept hearing someone trying to get into our room."

The headwaiter got the stonewall look only the British could pull off. "Probably someone from the convention on the first floor. They were in the bar until well after midnight. Probably someone lost their way and was trying to find their room."

"I can understand someone losing their way once or even twice, but all night?" I said, at the risk of sounding like the American bitch.

"I'm sure the management will make an adjustment on your account, madam." With a nod, he was off with no further comment.

As we got ready to leave, the busboy clearing a nearby table whispered to Charles, "Try the castle. They'll give you the whole story. This place is haunted, and that's God's truth."

Charles was going to shrug the whole thing off as a tourist trap. "It's done in England all the time. Get some poor sod to wander the castle halls, moaning and dragging chains, then play dumb when tourists complain, especially if the tourist is writing a guidebook. Probably the whole village is in on the dodge, including the castle."

"But we're tourists," I said. "Let's take the castle tour. You want to see the castle, Jeremy, right?"

Jeremy who usually would have to be chained to his chair at breakfast hadn't said a word during the whole conversation. He nodded. "Will the lady be there?"

"What lady?" we chorused.

My son looked from one of us to the other with round, mirthless eyes. "The one who came in my room last night."

That clinched it. We took the castle tour.

Charles took a ho-hum attitude as our guide, a friendly gent with a round, rosy face and bald spot, took Jeremy's hand, explaining how the castle grew from a keep that looked like a grain silo to the grim battlements around it.

Jeremy, delighted at not being mistaken for an insect or a ticking time bomb, skipped along beside him. "Does the lady in the white dress live here?"

The guide hesitated a few steps. He looked as if someone had just stuck him with a pin. "Who?"

Charles woke up enough to put the whole matter straight. "The boy probably had a dream last night about someone in a white dress coming into his room."

"I take it you stayed at The Royal Griffin last night, then?"

"And someone kept marching up and down the halls turning the door handle of Mommy's room and scared her, didn't he, Mommy?"

I felt all eyes looking at me as if to say it was all a bad dream, but was it really a dream? The guide got me off the hook. "You saw the ghost then, madam," he said as if it were fact not a question.

Charles sighed and looked skyward. "Probably just the roast lamb we had at dinner. Too much mint or some blasted thing."

"I can understand why your husband isn't impressed, madam. Men usually scoff and that's because the ghosts usually appear to women."

To Charles's disgust, I was hooked, even though his look told me I had fallen for the tourists' standard dodge. "Who is it the ghost of, do you know?"

Our Dickensian guide hesitated. "The whole history of the castle and village is in our gift shop below." Here Charles gave a snort of disgust. "But I'll just tell you it's a story not fit for young ears." He jerked his head toward Jeremy who was listening intently.

When we got off the battlements to the shelter of the dungeon, Jeremy ran ahead to look at the instruments of torture and the guide dropped back beside me. "The story goes," he said "that the young lady of the castle took her little son and ran off with a groomsman while the lord was away fighting in some battle or other. The couple hid in the inn, planning to leave at first light when the lord suddenly returned early and surprised them during the night. To say he butchered them would be an understatement. Suffice to say, the lord of the manor was tried for the double murders and let off with only a slap on the wrist for a crime of passion. He took the little boy back to the castle and so established the line of ascendancy, although the last direct descendant perished in World War I."

I shivered in the damp dungeon as a cold draft swept through the stone walls.

Back in London, I got access to a computer and typed in the only family name I could possibly determine was of Welch origin. Then, on a whim, I typed in Charles's surname. I was appalled to find out that way back in the 1400s, our genetic paths had crossed. A young Welch princess of fourteen had been married to a widowed English lord to solidify ties with England. A sacrificial lamb if there ever was one. Lady Lewellyn was one of the vast number of miserable girls in history used to seal a political tie with their bodies, but not with their hearts. The lady in white was trying to tell me that, though her dash for freedom had failed, her heart remained free. I left for New York the very next day.

Chapter 6

MISSION

It was spring and the days were getting warmer, signaling the end of school for Allison and her girlfriends. The girls longed for something wild and adventurous to happen in their humdrum lives, but all they could come up with was going to the Friday night movies to see who was there with who. As an added incentive to get the party started, one of the girls brought a pint of Jack Daniels to put in their super-sized sodas.

Her mom wasn't home from work yet, so Alison left a note on the kitchen table, explaining where she had gone and what time she'd be back. Approximately. Her mother probably wouldn't even care, she was so distracted by Jake's illness. Jake, Allison's older brother, had been diagnosed with a complicated form of hernia, requiring immediate surgery. Allison's father, a major in the army, was in Afghanistan training the Afghan Army. So the burden of responsibility of taking care of the family fell squarely on her mother's shoulders.

Allison felt a little guilty about not accompanying her mother to the hospital but, after all, a girl had to have some fun. Jake would understand that, even if her mom couldn't. In fact, she was probably cramping his style, knowing her brother's tendency to flirt with the pretty nurses.

So the five girls set out across the park, bound for the movie theater just on the other side. It was still light out, otherwise, Allison would have insisted on walking around the park to the movie theater. There had been two muggings and a girl, out jogging, had been raped recently. But there was comfort in numbers, and the five were not about to let their party mood be dampened.

They linked arms and sang at the top of their lungs, causing dogs to bark and skateboarders to detour around them. After getting sodas and popcorn, they were settled into their seats to watch an endless assortment of trailers before the featured film. The action on the screen suddenly suspended and a voice over of h the intercom said, "If Allison Porter is in the theater, would she please report to the service stand?"

Thinking her mother was having her paged, Allison transferred her drink and popcorn to the girls on either side of her and went up the aisle to the service stand where the manager was standing.

"I'm Allison Porter. Is there a problem?"

The manager said he had a message saying she had to return home right away, her mother would be waiting for her. Wondering why her mother hadn't called herself, she got out her cell phone and realized she had turned it off before going into the theater. Her mom's call was simply transferred to voicemail.

That worried her even more. Suppose there was something wrong with Jake? Maybe he had gotten worse and had to go into surgery right away? Thoughts were racing through Allison's mind like greyhounds after a rabbit when she realized she had started across the park and it was getting dark. No more skateboarding adolescents, no more joggers, no dog walkers. Where was everybody? She started to run, but that was a mistake. She was wearing her most ridiculous heels, the ones that made her walk teetering forward.

Not wanting to risk falling, Allison was forced to slow down and walk through the ever-darkening park, What was so familiar in the daytime became obscured in shadows as dusk deepened into twilight. Suddenly, she thought she heard someone softly call her name, a familiar voice from the bushes to her left. She tried to ignore that voice, telling herself it was just her imagination playing tricks in the dark.

Then her father stepped out of the bushes onto the grass. He was dressed in his uniform, his officer's cap under his arm, spit-and-polished to the max, as usual.

"Dad! I didn't know it was you! Didn't even dream it was you! Why didn't you tell us you were coming home? Have you seen Mom yet? And Jake's in the hospital. Come on, I'll take you there. Can't wait to see his face when I—"

Something strange about the fixed way her father was looking at her stopped Allison in mid-sentence. It as though he was looking straight through her. She tried to start again. "I know I should have been with Mom at the hospital—"

"Listen, Allie, I haven't got much time and there's somewhere else I have to be, so just listen, okay?"

Allison nodded. Her dad always didn't have much time and had to be somewhere else. She was used to that, but that didn't make it any easier.

"I want you to know I love you and your mother and Jake. And you have to take care of your mother. It'll be hard, but you can do it. And Jake's going to be fine. You'll see. Now, I've got to go. Be good, kitten, and know I'll always love you."

Her voice rose in a little-girl whine. "But can't you just walk with me to the house? Mom will be back any minute, and she wants to see you so bad."

His expression didn't change, but then, her father didn't talk much, even when he wasn't in a hurry. "Wish I could but I have to be somewhere else. Be brave, Allison."

Then she watched him disappear again into the shadows just beyond the trees. When she got to the house, a strange car was parked in the driveway behind her mother's car. One of her friend's accompanying her home from the hospital, probably, although all her mom's friends had jazzier cars than that.

Before she could unlock the front door, she heard her mother scream, "No, no, don't say that!" over and over again.

Allison rushed into the living room and found two uniformed army officers with desperate expressions on their faces. She had been an army brat for two long not to know what they were doing there, but putting the reality aside, she went to her mother's side. By that time, Mrs. Porter had slipped off the sofa and sat like a broken puppet on the living room floor, scratching her face until the blood ran.

"We took the liberty of calling her doctor," one of the officers said. "He'll be right over and give her something to calm her down."

"Your daddy is dead," her mother screamed. "He's not coming back ever again."

Allison sat down and clasped her mother's hands. Finding her father's words in her mouth, she stroked her mother's hair. "It's going to be all right, Mom. I'm going to take good care of you, and Jake's going to be fine. You'll see."

Chapter 7

THE HOUSE ON THE HILL

The Brysons knew it was going to be their house the minute they saw the stately old mansion, standing on the hill overlooking the town.

"You kind of expect the original owner to step out on the second floor veranda, smoking his cigar," Larry said.

"With a snifter of brandy in his hand," said his wife, Kelly. "Which is right where I want to be."

They were from New Jersey, where most of the grand old houses had disappeared to make way for bedroom communities.

"Probably needs some fixing up," said the realtor. "After all, it was built in 1855. Last owners were planning on flipping it to make a quick profit, but never finished what they started. Ran out of money, I heard. But if you're interested, I'm sure they'll make you a good price."

On closer inspection, the house was just as beautiful inside as the lush gardens around it—high ceilings with ornate molding, marble fireplaces, and a state-of-art kitchen. Larry had been moved to Atlanta by his company to open a new plant and was feeling flush. He made the owners a lowball offer, and they took it without a fight.

He and Kelly told their four kids that night they would love their new home. The next day, the kids didn't disappoint them, riding down the banister on the winding staircase and squabbling over which bedroom was theirs.

The older children chose the gabled rooms under the attic while four-year-old Molly stayed on the second floor near her parents.

Soon, the Brysons were caught up in the whirlwind of settling in—Larry with his new job, Kelly with decorating what seemed like a hotel, the kids with school. One night early in October, the noises began.

The children were awakened about midnight by what sounded like heavy footsteps overhead, followed by a rumbling noise. The youngest boy pulled his covers over his head and went back to sleep. But the oldest just stared at the ceiling, afraid to move. When he heard footsteps in the hall, he hid under the pillow, shaking so much the bed frame squeaked.

The next morning, Megan Bryson announced the house was haunted. "It sounded like someone was dragging something heavy across the attic floor," she said.

The boys just traded smirks, meaning "girls are loony." But their sister wasn't fooled.

"You two were hiding under the covers. I saw you!"

They were immediately on the defensive. "That means it was you making that noise just to scare us, pretending to be a ghost!"

"So you admit you heard it!"

"We heard you stumbling around is all!"

The squabbling continued until the school nurse called to say the oldest boy, Grey, had been falling asleep in class. "You live in the old McAllen place, right?" the nurse asked.

Kelly could hear something in the woman's voice, something that made her uneasy. "Yes, why do you ask?"

The nurse hesitated. "Nothing. It's just that, two years ago, I had a child in my infirmary who lived in that house. Same complaint as your son."

"I guess I don't understand," said Kelly. "What's my son complaining about?" She launched into every mother's disclaimer. "We've just moved in and, naturally, the kids have a hard time settling down—"

"I suggest you ask your boy what the problem is," the nurse said. Claiming her office was getting full, she hung up.

When Kelly arrived at school to pick up the children, Grey climbed in the SUV without a word. She thought he was in a bad mood because he had to make up what he had missed in class as well as homework. He threw a foul look at his sister as if it were all her fault.

After dinner, Kelly pulled him aside. "What did you tell the nurse when she asked you why you couldn't sleep at night, son?"

Grey stared down at the floor trying to hide his confusion. "That my sister loves teasing us, making noise during the night like—"

"Like?"

He raised his face and she could see the misery in his eyes. "Like a ghost."

Since Larry was working late these days, Kelly decided to settle the matter herself. She moved into the room next to her daughter's, evicting the three cats who complained bitterly.

The week of Halloween, exhausted from driving Mom's Taxi to football practice, dance lessons, and dentist appointments, Kelly crawled into bed in the spare room, ready for a good night's sleep. That wasn't what she got.

Close to midnight, she awoke to feel a cold draft coming from somewhere nearby. Old houses are drafty, she thought, putting insulation on her mental list to check out. Just then, a heavy footstep directly above her head turned her entire body to a solid block of ice.

Another footstep followed the first and then a dragging sound as if something heavy were being pulled across the attic floor overhead. Kelly was too scared to move until, mercifully, the footsteps faded as whatever it was went across the attic, dragging its awful load.

When she could move, Kelly fled into Megan's room to find her daughter sitting up in bed, wide-eyed, her finger to her lips. Kelly jumped in bed beside Megan, wrapping her arms around her. They were both shaking so violently, their teeth were chattering.

"I'm so sorry, honey." Kelly stroked her daughter's long hair. "We'll find out what's going on, I promise."

The Brysons held a family council to devise a plan to get rid of the "noisy ghost." Larry was no help. He slept in the spare room with the dogs and didn't hear anything. "Best night's sleep I've had since I came down from Jersey. Except for the dogs growling. But I shut 'em up, pronto."

Grey just kept eating his cereal.

But his younger brother said, "They always do that whenever the ghost comes."

Meanwhile, Kelly researched the county records and found the house had been built by a prosperous mill owner, Major Thomas McAllen. In the town library, in a slim volume of the town's history, the McAllens were listed among the town's leading families until 1864. Their house came under fire during the Battle of Atlanta, but escaped the bulk of Sherman's wrath. Major McAllen and his son were both killed during the Civil War and the house remained abandoned until a nephew took it over in 1871.

"Is there anyone that can tell me a little more history of the McAllen house?" she asked the reference librarian as she returned the book. "Like a longtime resident, maybe?"

He thought a minute and then scribbled name and number on a card. "This is the person you need to talk to."

It said *Minnie Harper, Psychic Tours.*

"Wait a minute, I meant someone reliable, not a tarot card reader."

"Oh, Minnie's reliable. A little touched in the head, but she knows everything about the town. Her family has lived here since God was a child. You live in the McAllen house, right? I saw it on your address card when you registered. It's on Minnie's tours, you know."

"Tours?"

"Minnie does ghost tours among other sightseeing attractions. Give her a call. I'm sure she'd love to meet you. "

When she got home, Kelly filed the card in the trash. At Christmastime, the house shone above the town, decorated so beautifully, the local paper featured it on the front page. When the Brysons saw the photo shoot, in every photo, there was a light in the attic even though the attic wasn't wired for lights.

By the time Spring came, the family had gotten used to their noisy ghost, nicknaming him Mr. Morlock. One day in February, Kelly heard her youngest child, Molly, chattering away in her room. Looking in, she saw the little girl making Valentines at her play table.

"No, not that way, Mr. Morlock. Watch the way I cut them out. See, it just takes practice, that's all."

"Who're you talking to, honey?"

Molly turned and saw her mother standing in the doorway. "Mr. Morlock, Mommy. Can't you see him? See, he's wearing a blue uniform. He says he's a Union soldier."

In March, Larry decided to put in a swimming pool. The perfect place was the rose garden, he said, and the contractor started to work. The second day, Larry got a call. It was the contractor. "I think you'd better call the police. There're some bones in your backyard and a human skull."

The headlines in the local paper said *Local Residence Yields Mystery Resident*.

The Bryson's backyard was wreathed in yellow tape, the swimming pool was put on hold until the coroner proclaimed there hadn't been a homicide: the bones were over 100 years old. An archeologist was called in to make certain they weren't Native American remains. However, he found some other things at the site that were clues to the identity of the remains. These included splinters of wood from the pine coffin, a gold wedding band, and a bit of dark blue cloth attached to gold braid. The ring was engraved with two names—Jacob and Agnes.

When the story appeared in the local paper, the Brysons got a phone call. "I always thought stories were just rumors," the caller said. "But it's really true." Then she backed up. "Hello, I'm Minnie Higgins and I'm going to tell you about your ghost.

"Stories about the McAllen house were handed down through generations," Minnie explained. "Some said it was the ghost of the Major himself, dragging his son's coffin across the attic in penance for ordering him into battle."

Kelly shook her head. "But, as the bit of cloth was dark blue, the archeologist identified it as belonging to a Union uniform."

"That makes more sense," said Minnie. "The other story I heard is that a wounded Yankee soldier took refuge in the house, hiding in the attic to escape from Confederate troops as they withdrew. When Sherman torched the city, the Yankee was too weak to escape, but the house was on a hill so it survived. Without food or water, the soldier eventually died. When the McAllen nephew came back in 1871, he found the corpse up in the attic. He dragged the coffin out to the garden and buried it."

"Do you think we could ask Mr. Morlock, that's what we call him, to go back to wherever he's from," Kelly asked.

"He wants to go home, I think. I'll see which Union units were involved in the siege of Atlanta, and who is missing named Jacob. Leave it to me. And I'll do it for free if you promise you'll let me lead a ghost tour through your house once a year. We just won't tell them there isn't a ghost anymore."

Two days later, Kelly Bryson got an e-mail from Minnie. Mr. Morlock was really Jacob Swenson from Applegrove, Wisconsin. The town council would be glad to re-inter his remains in their Civil War cemetery if the Brysons would ship him back. Before he left, Molly made a Valentine to put in the coffin. It said, "Dear Mr. Morlock, I will miss you. Love, Molly."

The light went out in the attic.

Chapter 8

THE FACE IN THE WATER

It began as a prank, a bit of horseplay that got carried too far. The boys in the class of 2015 were celebrating their high school graduation with a beer party at a lake on the edge of town. A girl wandered by, looking for the bathroom, and they got the bright idea to grab her and threw her in the lake. One-two-three, heave ho, in she goes! They thought the resulting splash was so funny, they decided to have another beer.

The water was dark and shallow near the shoreline, so no one was sure where she had landed. When she didn't surface, Luke Anderson dove in and searched the black, tepid water for any sign of the nameless girl. There were a lot of broken long necks, whiskey bottles, old tires, and just trash, but no girl.

Luke surfaced. "It's shallow here. No more than six feet. But it drops off real sharp-like. She could have rolled off the ledge, and into the current."

The current was from a powerful spring that fed the lake. The locals called it The Jet Stream and you had to be local to know what that referred to. The boys from the graduating Class of 2015 knew what that meant, and their hearts sank like stones skipped on the lake. The girl— they didn't even know what to call her—had just vanished.

It didn't start as a conspiracy. They all woke up with hangovers, except Luke, a nerd who didn't drink and was on the swimming team. Who invited him? they asked themselves. No one knew but he was the one who had searched for the girl. They waited for the news to broadcast a missing person's report. *Girl Missing During Picnic At Lake.* But it never came. They began to feel it was just a bad dream, a boozy nightmare, except for Luke who didn't drink.

Luke was the son of two ministers—god fearing, straight-laced people who would surely rat on them to the police. They respectively went off to college, or to their fathers' trades, vowing to blame it on Luke if worse came to worse.

"Yeah, I remember. Luke got drunk and tried to kiss that girl."

Everybody looked at Art Palmer, the creative one, the cool one. The one that was headed for Broadway after finishing college.

"Oh, yeah, I remember now." Dean Curry II, the son of Dean Curry the commercial developer, was another cool guy. With his shock of red curly hair and freckles, Dean was a lookalike for the British prince. "Yeah, yeah, and she got mad and ran off into the dark—it was pitch black by the lake, and she fell off the embankment."

"Or Luke pushed her off." All eyes shot to Motorhead. "Luke's not cool, guys. He can't take rejection. Big athlete, big ego." They took another hit off the joint Motorhead was passing around. "I say if it was anyone's fault, it was Luke's."

The others nodded, like that would solve it.

It didn't. Despite Luke's conscience, despite his enlisting into the military and being sent to the Middle East, he still harbored that secret—the secret of the drowned girl with no name until he lost her in the dark waters of all the civilian casualties of a internecine war.

When he finally got home, Luke was a mess. The god of his childhood had deserted him, allowing little children to die of starvation, woman in burkas to cringe when he offered them food—afraid of what he might demand in return. He had seen people beheaded; babies still alive left in the road to die, their little faces covered with flies and ants; body parts flying through a crowded market place, spraying blood all over the food, after a suicide bomber had blown himself up. America seemed like another planet with it thirty kinds of everything. It seemed surreal like a kind of joke. Like most returning vets, he had trouble sleeping. He was gripped by nightmares when he tried, some so bad he frightened his parents by screaming out loud.

Out on the lake, he finally got some peace. His dad kept a small sailboat out at the marina, and Luke would go out all day, not even bothering to fish, just vegging trying to make sense of the world. On the boat, drifting to the sound of the water lapping the sides of the boat, it was his idea of heaven after the desiccating desert winds.

He had dozed off when he realized that the wind was building up to storm level. Luke always loved a storm on the lake, the way it came rushing over the water, turning the normally glassy water to choppy waves. Putting the sail up and cranking up the motor, he headed for the marina some distance away. When he looked down at the water washing over the side of the boat as he knifed through the waves, he thought he saw a face—a girl's face, her hair streaming out like a mermaid's into clusters of seaweed, sightless eyes, staring at the dark sky. Then she disappeared below the waves. Just then the sail caught a strong gust of wind, causing the small boat to almost capsize. Hanging to the tiller, Luke threw his weight to the opposite side, righting the boat as it scudded toward the marina.

His depression deepened so that, at one point, he felt he was going to take his own life. In the middle of the night, he sought help in the ER and was put in the psychiatric ward under suicide watch. He had put the thought of the girl aside, thinking it was an illusion, that he was seeing things, a waking dream of the horrors he had witnessed.

They sent a psychiatric intern in to see him. A little older than Luke, he, too, had served in Iraq and Afghanistan. At last, finding someone who understood what he was going through, Luke opened up, pouring out the torrents of words in some kind catharsis.

"Why did you enlist in the first place? You didn't have to. You had a full scholarship to a good university, a girlfriend, friends. Why did you throw all that stuff away?"

"Why did you?"

The doctor shrugged. "It paid for medical school."

Luke told him about the girl at the lake, how she wandered by asking the way to the bathroom and the guys had thrown her into the lake.

"But you didn't have anything to do with it. You tried to save her. So why do you feel guilty?"

"Because..." Luke searched and finally found the words. "Nobody seemed to care. No death should go unnoticed like that. I've seen so much in Afghanistan, seen so many people die. Unrecognizable bodies piled up. Just so anonymous."

"Why didn't you tell the police? They could have followed up on her." Seeing Luke's anguished face, the doctor let up on him. "I know. At that age you don't want to rat on your buddies. After all, they tossed her in the lake, you didn't. You even tried to rescue her." He looked at his watch. "Look, I've got a shitload of patients to see. Tell you what. When the chief gives you the okay to get out of here, go down to the library and ask the reference librarian for the newspapers of that date and the week afterward. Somebody had to miss her when she didn't come back from the bathroom. See if you can find out her name, something about her. Age, hair color, weight, anything. Then tell the police you're looking for her. See if they come up with anything. Who knows? It could turn out that she climbed out of the lake in the dark and went back to wherever she came from."

"Then why did I see her in the lake?"

"I don't have an answer for that. Maybe it was a waking dream, maybe you got imagination mixed up with reality. Like you said, you've seen a lot of death."

Luke followed the doctor's advice. He checked with the local police, but they said their digital records didn't go back that far. A detective looked the girl up on the FBI's Missing Persons' List but, not knowing her name, he couldn't identify her. The detective said there were any number of teenage girls on the Missing Persons' List.

In despair, Luke consulted the reference librarian at the local library about viewing the newspapers of that year on microfiche. There was one lone article about a missing girl named Carol Fleming who was attending a church picnic with a group from The Lutheran Children's Home.

Luke made a copy of the paper and contacted the home. Yes, they had a girl by that name go missing that year, but it was assumed she had run away because she had tried to run away several times before she went missing, but the police had always found her and brought her back. They had just figured she had succeeded this time.

"Are you a relative of Carol's?" the secretary asked.

Luke said he wasn't, just somebody she had gone to school with, and hung up, suddenly scared he would be accused of killing her. He made an appointment to see the psychiatrist again, and was surprised at how early he got in to see him, the VA being notoriously slow, especially their psychiatric departments.

"Well, did you find her?" The young doctor looked tired, as though he had been up all night. Luke told him the story. "And did you call the police back when you found out her name?"

Luke admitted he was too frightened, in case the police suspected him of foul play.

"Look, you've got to forget about it and go on with your life. You have nothing to feel guilty about. I wish all my cases were all as simple as yours. The trouble is what weighs on your conscience the most is the fact that you didn't tell somebody back then. Believe me, we all have things we should have done but didn't because we were afraid. Your service in the Middle East just exacerbates that feeling of guilt, and there were probably some things you did or should have done over there but didn't, right? But every one of us had to make decisions and some had to be made in a split second, like you diving in to save the girl. Let's face it, you could have been killed if the water was as shallow there as you described. Or crippled for life because you could have broken your neck. But you did it, anyway, without thinking about that. It was only an afterthought that you should have told someone about it. Accept that you're telling somebody now, and leave it at that. The girl is probably living somewhere with a husband and ten kids."

Luke got on with his life, got a girlfriend, and a job. He was watching the evening news when they pulled a body out of the lake. Or what was left of a body that had been snagged on a wrecked boat at the bottom. It was a young female—the ends of the bones hadn't stopped growing yet so they guessed she was about sixteen.

The Lutheran Home determined it was the remains of Carol Fleming whom they'd reported missing on the day of Luke's graduation. The coroner said she had drowned, an apparent suicide. She buried in the cemetery of the Lutheran church and each year a bouquet of white roses was placed on headstone with the words *I'm sorry* written on the note that accompanied it.

Chapter 9

ANDERSONVILLE

When I was a little kid, I heard my father exclaim, "Andersonville? That was a disgrace to the South and we ought to be ashamed that it happened here in Georgia."

When I asked my mother what Andersonville was, she just told me it was a prison camp during the Civil War and not to mention it to my dad. It would only make him mad and, since no one wanted to do that on purpose, I didn't find out what happened there until twenty years later.

A friend and I were driving back from the coast after spending a week on the beach. We were going west, chasing the sun as it dropped lower and lower over the rolling country inland, when we passed a sign that said *Andersonville Memorial Cemetery seven miles.*

"Want to take a little detour?" I asked.

She shrugged. "Sure. Why not? Don't tell me you've got a thing for cemeteries."

I told her what my dad had said about Andersonville being a disgrace to the South. "I just wanted to see why. Have they pushed over gravestones? Graffitied 'The South Will Rise Again' on the walls?"

My beach buddy wasn't into history. "Cemeteries give me the creeps," she said. "But you won't be happy until you see it, so let's go. It'll be getting dark soon. Then I'll really get creeped out."

"Then let's break out that bottle of vodka we brought back from the beach and spike our soda with it. We've got a bag of chips and some leftover dip back in the cooler. They've got to have picnic tables and a public bathroom way out here in the boonies. We'll make Andersonville a little bathroom and booze break, how's that?"

But as we got nearer to the cemetery, a silence fell between, us as though the shadows, that were looming over the road, had crept into the car, crouching there between us like some invisible ogre. When we did speak, it was in hushed monosyllables, as if someone would overhear us. There were picnic tables just inside the big stone walls where *ANDERSONVILLE* was spelled out in capital letters on both sides of the entry way. Since it was growing dark, there was no one else around, although loaded trash cans testified to a brisk business earlier in the day.

We left the car, bringing the cooler with us as we searched for a table that the birds hadn't decorated. Finally, we found one that had managed to capture the last of the sunlight filtering through the live oaks and gray fingers of Spanish moss.

We each opened a can of soda, sweetened it with vodka, got a handful of chips, and got back into the car to look for the bathroom, leaving the cooler on the table along with the bag of chips and several bottles of water.

The bathroom in the Welcome Center was clean, despite the number of cars lingering in the parking lot. As I waited for Jilly to buy postcards, I found what the disgrace was my dad was talking about. Like the western sun on the horizon, it blinded me briefly after I read the dedication at the entrance—fourteen thousand men had died here within thirteen months, Union prisoners in a Confederate Army camp. I did the math. That was a little over a thousand deaths a month!

My friend was cruising on vodka, and I tried to tell her what was out there before we walked to the first monument. But she just waved me off. "Let's get this over with and get back on the road. I'm starving for some of that fried chicken your mom makes."

The thought of food absolutely curdled my stomach. I dropped my unfinished chips and soda can in a trash basket. On a piece of pasture land this small, how had forty-thousand-something men survived? They hadn't.

With little groups of die-hard visitors, we walked to first monument and the next and the next, all with names of soldiers from different states. They survived the horrible slaughter of battles, just to die here of thirst, dysentery, and starvation. People moved as though in a dream from one monument to the next, talking in hushed voices as though they were feeling the same burden of guilt for just being alive as I was.

Jilly grew more and more agitated. "We'd better make this the last one. Unless that's a bathroom there."

"Didn't you go up there in the Welcome Center?"

We looked behind us at the distant building.

"I didn't have to, then. Besides, there was a line."

"Okay, let's walk down there." I pointed to a small stone building at the bottom of the hill. "Maybe there a bathroom's in there."

There wasn't. There was basin of water in the floor with a sign above it warning people that the water was not fit for human consumption.

"Eeew, who would want to drink from that horse trough anyway?" Jilly walked outside and threw her soda can away. "I'm going back, Ann. You come when you're ready, okay? I have really got to pee."

I nodded, stunned into silence. We were in the presence of a miracle. A miracle that happened over a century and a half before. The plaque above the small basin gave the account of what happened on this very spot in June 1864.

The prison camp at Andersonville was packed to four times its capacity with Union prisoners. They were living in their own excrement, dying of scurvy and thirst and disease bred by filth. It hadn't rained in days and rain was what they relied on to cool their bodies and fill their canteens with clean water in the Georgia heat.

Finally, a group of prisoners led by a chaplain got together to pray for rain and took an oath not to stop until their prayers were answered. Many were walking skeletons, many were too weak to stand and had to carried, but they all came anyway while the chaplain led the service. They took turns an hour at a time, praying in shifts, for almost two months. On August 8, 1864, clouds began to form and it rained lightly down on the parched camp. For the next five days, that rain became a torrent, washing away one wall of the stockade. The guards fired over the heads of the prisoners, in case anyone thought about escaping, but no one did. The excrement and filth were washed away into the little creek that ran through the camp.

The men held out anything they could catch the rain in—tin cups, bowls, canteens. Some just opened their mouths and let the sky give them their first taste of clean water. Then on August fifteen, a cloud as black and big as a mountain appeared, hovering over the camp. A lightning bolt like a cannon shot down from the cloud and there was explosion on the ground. The ground opened and, in the words of an eye-witness, "A spring of purest crystal shot up into the air in a column and, falling fanlike, spray came babbling down the grade into the noxious Stockade Creek. Looking across the dead-line, we beheld with wandering eyes and grateful hearts the fountain spring." John L. Maile, Eighth Michigan Infantry, August 15, 1864.

I walked back through the cemetery. The lights had come on and it wasn't half as gloomy as it had been in the twilight. Jilly was waiting in the Welcome Center, noshing on some salted nuts and chatting up some boy who was probably as bored as she was. We rode back to our picnic table which fortunately was under a street lamp. A ring of lacey mosquitoes danced around thje halo of light, reminding me of what it must have been like before repellent was invented.

When we went to get our cooler and water bottles, only the cooler was untouched. The water was gone and the bag of chips. In its place was Jilly's soda can—an exotic brew she had thrown half full in the trash can at Providence Spring. I remembered that she had tossed it in the can all crumpled up. But it sat in the puddle of light from the lamp as if it were newly minted, but empty like a reprimand to a generation that didn't know the value of a drop of rain.

Jilly took it in stride. "Huh, someone likes the same kind of soda I do," she said. "They could have left the chips, though. Something about this place makes me ravenous."

Chapter 10

YESHE

She struggled up the icy mountain, her breath freezing in the air. Half way up to the first cave, a fit of coughing racked her thin body. Yeshe coughed up blood on the snow. Red on pure white crystals. Sitting down in the snow, she looked down on the valley below to the place where, as a Buddhist nun, she lived in relative comfort. Relative as compared to the people living in the caves above her on the steep sides of the Himalayas. Tibetan refugees fleeing the Chinese takeover of their villages and monasteries were living there, unwilling to mix with the population of India yet in view of the Dalai Lamas's headquarters. Yeshe recovered her strength enough to keep going—up, up the side of the mountain to the first cave. Then she collapsed, just short of her destination.

The men of the first cave carried her and the heavy pack she had strapped to her back into the cave where a fire pit was burning. Laying Yeshe beside the fire, they brewed warm yak milk from the animal kept tethered outside and mixed with the chai tea leaves they found in her backpack.

Soon she felt strong enough to distribute the contents of her backpack to the waiting people of cave number one and move on to cave number two.

Yeshe was a Buhddist nun, dedicated by her devout family at age six. They had fled Tibet when was she was five, and her mother had crossed the Himalayan mountains that summer carrying her baby brother while Yeshe and her older brother had walked. Her father had stayed behind to defend their village, and they had never heard from him again. Her mother was forced to give up Yeshe and her brother to the Buddhist temple to keep them from dying of starvation.

Twenty years later, Yeshe had taken a vow not to let that happen to the people still living in the caves above the city. They were Tibetans, country people who farmed for a living. A proud people, they didn't like congested East Indian cities or East Indians who made fun of them because they didn't speak the language. The Tibetans sheltered their animals in mountain pastures and, in winter, they brought the animals into their caves as part of the family. The animals' droppings fueled their fires, keeping them warm during the fierce winters.

Most days, she carried more than food—medicine, books, jackets, boots, even toys which set the children twittering like little birds, not knowing what to do with them. On this day, when the wind was howling around the cliffs, blowing snow in blinding clouds, Yeshe felt her body giving out at the second cave. The residents of that cave, three generations of one family, a total of twelve people, made room for her by the fire. They spread their own mats to make her more comfortable. After drinking a bowl of ox tail soup, she fell into a feverish sleep.

The following day, they sent a boy down to the monastery below to get the monks to come help Yeshe descend the mountain, but the weather got worse, making climbing impossible.

By the time the weather cleared, Yeshe had recovered enough to make the journey down on her own. When she got back to the monastery, she endured a scolding from the head monk for her dereliction of duty.

"You were told not to go up there and you did it anyway. Therefore, you disobeyed my instructions."

Yeshe remained in postulant position, stretched out on the warm tiles of the monastery floor. She could have lain there forever, she thought. "Yes, Rimpoche."

As there were no excuses tolerated, she was set to scrubbing floors, keeping total silence. That was all right with Yeshe. She didn't have enough strength or breath to scrub and talk at the same time. As she scrubbed, she made plans for what she would bring when she climbed to the caves again.

The trouble was she needed medication, not for herself but for a sick child in the first cave who had a cough like hers. Only Yeshe couldn't ask the monks for a child's dose. That would set off alarm bells, and Rimpoche would even be more furious with her. So she decided to cut her own medication in half, there by doubling the quantity she would take with her.

When she had collected enough donations from the Tibetan community which lived and worked in the city surrounding the monastery, Yeshe made her journey up the mountain again.

It was during this trip, when spring was showing through the melting snow, that Yeshe didn't return to the monastery. The cave community found her lying face down in the snow in a pool of blood that some say looked like a heart. They carried her up to an empty cave and built a dung fire to keep her warm. Someone remained with her day and night, keeping the fire going, and taking turns to bring her food. Finally, she sat up and took some nourishment.

From then on, Yeshe remained in the cave, praying day and night. A delegation of monks made the climb up to the cave, marveling that such a sick person had climbed so far in the Himalayan Mountains, the most forbidding in the world. The villagers dared not tell them she had often carried over one-and-a-half times her weight in supplies, for fear of getting her in trouble.

The monks tried to persuade Yeshe to come down with them to the hospital in Delhi where she could get treatment for her tuberculosis, but she refused. "The mountain has restored my health," she told them, "and the kindness of the cave dwellers. So I will remain with them." She didn't rebuke them for making her scrub floors, but they hadn't been kind to her, and she could tell by their eyes that they knew it.

Yeshe's cave became the center for healing in the cave community. Sick people, crippled people, mad people, all came to Yeshe to find remedies to relieve their suffering, and she gave them the benefit of her extensive knowledge of herbal and dietary remedies for diseases. Many were healed and word spread across the mountains that there was a healer among them. Yeshe was kept busy from dawn to dusk, interrupting her busy schedule only for prayers. Often, her rest was interrupted because a pregnant woman was in trouble or a child had been taken ill in the middle of the night. Yeshe always went to them, carrying her medicine bag with her.

One morning, after the first snowfall of winter, someone noticed there was no smoke coming from Yeshe's cave. They discovered her fire had gone out during the freezing night, and Yeshe was sitting in prayer posture against the cave wall. Her body was still warm and supple, but her heart had stopped beating. She had deliberately let the fire go out, sitting there watching—as one by one, like the minutes of her life, the embers, were extinguished.

They buried Yeshe on her the mountain in an unmarked grave. Nevertheless, the cave people knew exactly where the spot was and often brought offerings there. In the spring, a plant sprang up on spot where Yeshe was buried—a healing herb thought to be long extinct that soon covered the area. The herb had a reputation for curing the rotting sickness known in the West as cancer.

Word got to the monastery below and the monks began to harvest the herb, trying to cultivate the plant in their gardens. But Yeshe's herb—that's what the cave people called it—would only grow on the side of the high Himalayan mountain she loved. None of the monks knew that was where Yeshe was buried, but they noticed the bowls of offerings and guessed. One day, a monk climbed to what had been Yeshe's cave. Even though there were more and more refugees from Chinese-occupied Tibet in the area, he saw the cave wasn't being used by a family. Instead, the cave had been turned into a kind of shrine, with sick people laying on pallets, tended by Yeshe's pupils, the ones she had instructed in herbal medicine and the importance of cleanliness in fighting disease. The cave was clean and warm, and, as the monk stood in the opening, a girl came up to him and asked what his ailment was.

He thought of half a dozen things he could say, but instead of making up an excuse for being there, he simply said, "I'm looking for Yeshe's shrine so I can gain wisdom."

"You are looking at Yeche's shrine," the girl answered. "It is the service we give to the dying and the healing of the sick. As Yeshe taught us, 'as we work, we learn.' That is our offering to Yeshe."

The monk went down the mountain to the head of the monastery and told him what the girl had said.

"Rubbish! Those mountain girls know nothing about healing the sick," the head monk said. "Yeshe was an ignorant girl, unfit to instruct anyone on the art of medicine. What could she possibly know, a Tibetan girl from a small village across the mountains?"

Time passed, and the path to Yeshe's cave became worn with the feet of the desperate-to-be-healed. Some said the spirit of Yeshe moved among the sick and dying at night, healing as she passed. A man, blind since birth, slowly regained his sight. The crippled threw away their crutches.

The rumors rumbled like boulders in an avalanche into the monastery at the bottom of the mountain.

"Rubbish! Nothing that can't be accomplished by good care and nutrition," the old and wise among them said.

One morning, however, a strange image appeared as the sunlight briefly reached the back of Yeshe's cave. There, on the rock wall where she used to sit in adoring meditation, was an image of a tall slender woman like Yeshe herself had been. On hearing this, the monks climbed the mountain in a saffron stream to the cave. They brought incense, wine, and food to make *puja*. Instead of making an offering, the nuns insisted they distribute the food and wine among the patients. "Because that's what Yeshe would want you to do."

So the monks did as they were told. After blessing the libations, they set about distributing them among the grateful patients, many of whom had never tasted such fine food before. After they returned to the monastery, the head monk who hadn't made the pilgrimage rebuked them for following the nuns' suggestion.

"That libation was meant to make *puja* to Buddha, If you were going to do that with it, you should have taken just rice and tea, not our finest wine, goat cheese, and meat! That's not even good for sick people!"

The youngest monk, a mere slip of a boy, said, "But Rimpoche, the Buddha himself turned away from such rich food because he said the poor couldn't eat like him so he was going to eat like the poor. I think the nuns were just giving Buddha's food to the poor."

He ended up scrubbing the floor for two months. "Some people never learn to be humble," the monks all said.

Chapter 11

MR. ANGEL

He was a small, balding man, coming barely up to my shoulder. He appeared beside me at The American Club bar, a place where ex-pats gathered in Greece to lament their misfortune at having been assigned to an island originally meant for goats. He didn't sit down and used a bar stool as a desk to sort out stacks of papers.

"I'm selling insurance," he said. "My name is hard for Americans to pronounce so just call me Mr. Angel."

"Sure, why not?" After a couple of glasses of wine, you could have sold me the Agora, or Temple of Venus, or even the Parthenon, a scam the Greeks had probably pulled on the Romans back in BC. "What kind of insurance? If it's life, my husband took out a million on me a long time ago. I think he's been trying to bump me off ever since."

Mr. Angel appreciated the joke with an easy laugh. "I hear that a lot, even from Greek women. Is your husband in the oil business?"

"Does it show that much?"

He shrugged. "You could be in the military, stationed at the missile base."

"We get paid more and protected less. When we're evacuated and have to live in strange places, we don't have a commissary handy either. Those are the major differences between oil and the military."

"So you've been evacuated from…"

"Riad. Not him. He's still dodging missiles in the Gulf. Just me and the two boys and about fifty other people. When I was offered either Cyprus or Greece, I thought why not see the islands and the temples? What I didn't know is a million other people had the same idea. Only they decided to swim over. So I have no room to complain. I flew first class."

"No." Suddenly intent on shuffling his papers, Mr. Angel looked so sad, I thought he was about to cry. "They have no life insurance either. Not even life jackets."

Like every other Athenian, I realized, Mr. Angel had seen the plight of the refugees. Maybe he had even tried to sell them insurance.

My friend came back from chatting with almost everyone in the room. "Hi, Mr. Angel. How is the insurance business going?"

His face lit with a broad smile. "Ah, beautiful lady! How are you getting along, Mrs. Chelsea?"

My friend Chelsea, whose husband was with the American Embassy, was better at diplomacy than her husband was and better-looking, as well. "Selling Lara here some insurance? Believe me, Lara, it can't do any harm to buy insurance in Greece. You never know, do you? What may happen, I mean."

Mr. Angel and Chelsea traded glances and they nodded in unison. "That's true," said Mr. Angel. "One never knows."

"And you'll be contributing to the Greek economy. That's two good reasons."

"You should sell insurance, Chelsea. I bet you'd make a million dracmas, at least."

"In that case, I won't bother. Come on, let's get you home to the boys. Peter's probably going mad with the four of them running around."

I bought Mr. Angel's full package of Greek auto insurance for ten dollars a month, payable in US dollars, and went home with Chelsea. Her husband Pete was reading a newspaper in the living room while their cook, Mustafa, played with the boys. The Grahams had brought him from Cairo, but he was from the Sudan and wore a turban as his fellow tribesman did. The boys had wrapped towels around their heads and were reenacting Lord Gordon's stand against the Maadi, Mustafa playing the part of the Maadi. My youngest, Michael who was three, sat on the stairs with the towel around his head and face, avoiding the sound of fake gunfire.

The next morning, it was my turn to drive the carpool for the kindergarten crowd and drop Michael off at pre-school where he was learning to speak Greek. I picked three more ex-pat children besides my own. They all were glad to have a routine, after being shuttled from country to country like so many pieces of luggage. While making my rounds, I noticed the clear morning sky becoming dark with scudding clouds. A storm was coming in from the vast Mediterranean Sea, boiling up from some cauldron where the sea monsters lurked in Greek myths. By noon, waiters were whipping white table cloths off of outdoor tables before they blew into the traffic. Shop keepers were rescuing large flower pots as they turned over, dumping dirt and plants all over the sidewalk. Anything not anchored down became a missile, an umbrella a sail.

Michael's pre-school was out at twelve-thirty and, by the time, kindergarten let out at one, a full-scale storm had hit the mountains and the suburb where we lived. Torrents of rain battered people waiting at bus stops. Eventually, I emerged from sluggish traffic and, with the car at a fifteen-mile-per-hour crawl, headed down a wide boulevard on my way to drop the first child off. It was raining so hard, it seemed as if someone was standing on the roof of the car, pouring garbage cans of water over my windshield. I barely caught a glimpse of a figure carrying an umbrella running across the boulevard. I couldn't tell whether it was a man or a woman since the umbrella was lowered over their face like a shield. Slowing to a stop, I laid on the horn but the person kept the umbrella in front of their face against the driving rain.

"Mommy, she isn't stopping!" Matthew, my oldest boy, shouted as she ran into the street.

The black umbrella skidded across the hood of my car as the woman holding it collided with the passenger side door. She looked into the car window and saw the children looking back at her. She retrieved her umbrella and, mumbling apologetically, backed up to the curb.

Any ex-patriot living broad especially in the Mediterranean countries would tell you not to get out of the car when involved in a traffic accident, especially in the Arab countries. It had cost some well-meaning drivers their lives. Just phone the police and wait in the car, doors locked.

Ignoring every rule in the guide books, I got out of the car and, in Greek, asked the woman if she was all right. She took one look at me, another at the stony faces of the children in the car, and began questioning me. "English? Alemani?"

I shook my head.

"Amerikaniya?"

I nodded and she immediately sat down on the curb in the pouring rain and began to rock back and forth, moaning. The game was on. I offered to take her to the hospital to let a doctor check her out. My second mistake. The woman got into the car. I dropped the kids off at the first house in the car pool, and took her to the hospital where a doctor found her fit for running a marathon.

He smiled at me. "But I wouldn't give her your name, if I were you. If you do that, she'll probably come up with every ailment known to mankind."

Picking up the boys, I took them home and had a large glass of wine, then called Chelsea, my friend married to the diplomat. "You acted nobly, but foolishly. You know better and yet you got involved anyway, you bloody-minded creature!"

I was hoping for sympathy, but she sounded so cross, I was a little worried. "But she was obviously poor, an older woman about fiftyish. I couldn't just leave without seeing if she was okay. What kind of example would that have been for the kids? And, for that matter, as an American? We're on sketchy terms with the Greek government anyway."

"Um…" was Chelsea's reply. "Got to dash, pet. Call you tomorrow."

Next thing I knew, a police car—I hadn't even seen one since we had arrived six months earlier—pulled up in front of the house. The driver got out, opening the door for the officious one in back. He got out, surveyed the house the company had rented for duration of the evacuation, and strode down the garden walk.

It turned out that woman that the woman had gone straight to the police station after I left the hospital and charged me with running her down. The police chief spoke perfect English, having grown up in Chicago. Captain Popadopalus and his driver took down my statement while recording me on his cell phone, admired the two boys who came in to sit beside me on the couch.

When they left, Matt asked, "Mommy, are they going to take you away?"

I assured them that the police were just asking questions, but in the morning, they did just that. What followed was a blur of being fingerprinted in the main port of Piraeus along with prostitutes and their pimps who conjured up lawyers a lot quicker than I did. One man in an impeccable silk suit even offered me his services, apparently all of them.

"What are your charges? Drugs, is it? I can get you off easily for a hundred American dollars for me and another hundred for my friend here," he said, nodding and winking at the man taking my finger prints.

"That won't be necessary." We both looked around to see Mr. Angel standing there.

"Ah, the insurance salesman," sneered the lawyer and, without another word, melted into the crowd of the police roundup of the night.

With a few words to the fingerprint man, Mr. Angel took me by the elbow and steered me back out of the police station to a waiting car.

"This is Mr. Agnelli and he will represent you in court." At Mr. Angel's direction, I got in beside the Greek god in the Saville Row suit who smiled at my confusion.

"Court?"

"Have you had coffee yet?"

By now, I was familiar with how business was conducted around the Mediterranean. It usually involved coffee, some sort of food, and time, lots of time. The first thing I did when I returned home was to call Chelsea. Mustafa answered, "Mrs. Lara? Mrs. Chelsea says she is out."

That was my first clue I could count the American Embassy out as far as help was concerned. Chelsea had the grace to call me back and apologize for Mustafa's poor English, but I knew Mustafa had heard her right. She confirmed that when she said "Peter can't be involved, you know? Not in civil matters involving American citizens."

I started to ask her what the hell the Embassy was there for if not to help their own countrymen since they were supported by taxpayer dollars, but apparently, Chelsea knew it was coming. "Got to run, pet. Let me know how it all turns out, will you?" she said and hung up.

One snowy day in early winter, I found myself in a Greek court with Mr. Angel, the Greek god, and Mr. Angel's sister who would interpret for me what was going on. That week I had just gotten word that my case had coincided with the news that the United States ban on traveling in the Middle East had been lifted. I was free to take the children back to Riad where my husband was stationed.

The court was held in a partially roofed building, sometimes allowing swirls of snowflakes that rained down on defendants and prosecutors alike. The judges and everyone else in the packed court were bundled up in overcoats, hats, and scarves. Some were even wearing gloves. The first case, I gathered, was a child custody hearing in which everyone talked at once, standing in front of the judges' bench—lawyers, mother, father, grandmothers, and granddads, all in a cacophony of strident voices, each one trying to make their point by out-shouting the others. The judges remained stoically nodding as if they had deciphered every word. Then one banged his gavel down and spoke. The whole lot cleared out, leaving the child, a small boy alone. The judges leaned forward, exchanging a few words with him. The gavel banged again. The lead judge spoke again and a great cheer went from the packed courtroom.

An old woman obviously disagreed, and waving her cane to emphasize her displeasure, advanced on the judges' bench while giving them a lecture in a shrill voice. The judges listened without expression to the old lady's diatribe. When she took a wheezing breath, the lead judge spoke and a security guard escorted the woman back to her seat, still flailing her cane and ranting angrily.

Our turn was next and a hush fell over the whole courtroom as the Greek god presented his case in such a suave manner, I noticed several ladies fanning themselves. Next the claimant's lawyer presented his client's case and passed the judge a large envelope. I could tell without Mr. Angel's sister translating that those were X- rays. The judges passed them along the bench, smiling. Then the lawyer called the woman with the black umbrella to stand in front him and the lawyer brought her forward, leaning on his arm and limping. She pointed at me and said in Greek that was the American lady who had run her down as she was crossing the street. She then pretended to swoon, hand to forehead Greta Garbo style, into her lawyer's arms. I noticed he was right there to catch her.

The whole court gasped and someone giggled. Even I could tell she was faking it, but then, I couldn't tell about judges' reaction. I looked at Mr. Angel. He had an archaic smile on his cherubic face.

Then it was my turn to take the stage.

Mr. Angel leaned over and whispered, "Remember what I told you. Don't speak unless to answer their questions, and remember to say in Greek, '*metaferoun mia mavri omprela*' and don't cross your legs."

The lead judge was smiling as he motioned me forward. There was a murmur rippling through the courtroom as I went up and stood before him.

His first question took me wholly by surprise. "What does your father do?" he said in perfect English.

Not seeing what that had to do with anything, I stammered, "W—why, he's a writer and a professor," which was the truth. I didn't dare say anything else because I knew that they would have a complete file on me by now.

"In your own words, tell the court what happened on the day in question,"

As Mr. Angel had instructed, I gave a concise account of driving the kids to school, the storm, and ended with a description of the woman "*metaferoun mia mavri omprela*," carrying a black umbrella. I must have got it right because nobody laughed and there were nods of approval among the judges.

Second question. "And did you stop the car before she collided with your automobile?"

I said I had. He conferred with the other judges and then said something harsh in Greek to the woman's lawyer who stood up to receive the rebuke. I didn't have to know much Greek to understand what the judge was saying. Something to the effect of her trying to hoodwink the court and make a mockery of Greek justice. Above all, wasting the court's time as well as dragging this poor mother of five children to court when she should be home looking after them. And furthermore, if he ever showed up before this judge again, he would have the lawyer disbarred.

The courtroom erupted in cheers and applause. The poor attorney looked like a tree struck by lightning. I was surprised his hair wasn't on fire. The snow poured down like a blessing from the clouds. I thanked the judge in my best Greek accent, but I don't think he heard me. In fact, he was obviously so angry, he seemed to have forgotten I was standing there in front of him. Looking around at Mr. Angel and his crew, I caught them all smiling and the Greek god making a gesture to the fallen attorney that in any language meant "up yours."

The confusion lasted until the judge banged his gavel tree times and the room was quiet except for the street noises. "Young lady, I know you have very little idea what has just happened, but I want you as American to be proud to tell your father you have seen Greek democracy in action. Several witnesses have come forward and sworn the woman only collided with your car after running full tilt into the street. They have also said your car was fully stopped when she collided with it. Her attorney has just produced a series of X-Rays showing tire tracks across her entire rib cage. Fool!" This directed at the dejected lawyer who probably wouldn't get paid, judging from the dirty looks his client was giving him. "If those films were true, she would be dead and not be bothering the court with ludicrous antics! But she is a poor woman who works in hotels as a maid. So, if you will be good enough to pay thirty dollars for her hospital visit, you are free to go. I wish you luck."

Before I could go back to my seat, the old lady from the child custody case stood up and advanced toward the stricken lawyer waving her cane and giving him hell. Before the security guard could catch up with her, she had given the poor lawyer several good whacks which sent him running to a side door.

The court adjourned and we beat a hasty retreat, following the crowd out the door. Once on the street, we lost the Greek god in the crowd, no doubt because he was going to beat his fallen opponent to a pulp. But I saw them behind us, arm in arm as if they were going for a few beers. Mr. Angel's sister kissed me on both cheeks and said she had another trial after lunch which meant at four o'clock.

Mr. Angel started to jog ahead of me and I caught up with him though I was wearing heels. "What's the hurry?"

"We have to run quick in case the judges change their minds," he said. "We are meeting your children at the airport." Mr. Angel produced an airplane ticket from somewhere in his raincoat pocket. "Just get directly on the plane. I've sent your luggage on ahead." That was when I learned that my name was on the No Fly list as a wanted criminal.

Chelsea was at the airport with the boys, although I had left them at home in the charge of the cleaning woman. They both broke free of her hands and came running when our driver let me out at the curb. An hour before, I had thought that I wouldn't be seeing them or feeling their arms around me for a very long time. I was just content to hold them now when Mr. Angel said, "You'd better get on the plane. The pilot's waiting for you." Bowing, he kissed my hand. "Adieu, Lara. You would have made very good student of Socrates."

"Except he drank the hemlock."

I meant it as a joke, but Mr. Angel looked solemn without his usual cherubic smile.

"Exactly. But you didn't. There is always something to live for."

Chelsea came hurrying over and walked with me across the tarmac to the waiting prop jet. At the bottom of the ramp, she stopped. "I mustn't be seen. Peter will have a lot of explaining to do, as it is. Safe journey, pet. Write when you can, but please send it by courier." Kissing me on both cheeks, she whispered close to my ear, "When two countries play football, sometimes individuals get kicked around, know what I mean? You can't take it personally, pet." Gripping my face with both hands, Chelsea looked at me, her eyes filled with tears. "Mm, so pretty. Promise you'll write, pet. Must dash."

My last glimpse of her as I boarded the plane was as she hurried away without looking back. I never heard from her again. Chelsea and her husband were both killed when the American embassy was bombed in Africa, where they had just been posted.

Chapter 12

DEER WOMAN

Driving was normally tough on the Interstates across northern Iowa. In winter, it was plain awful with black ice, blinding snow, and drivers slowing down almost to a halt while others swerved to avoid them, often losing control of their cars. It was even worse when there were kids in the car, Ed thought, squabbling over a bag of chips.

His twelve-year-old son, Lyle, was riding shotgun in the passenger seat of family SUV playing a game on his tablet, ignoring the clamor in the back seat. Ed was listening to the weather report as it became worse and worse. His car phone rang and Ed put the speaker on. It was Myrna, his wife.

"Maybe you'd better turn back," she said.

They'd been married long enough for him to detect the worry in her voice. They'd both been raised in Iowa and knew that the hockey game would never be cancelled for a foot or even the forecast for more. Plus Lyle and Mac's heart were set on it. Malcolm usually warmed the bench, but he wouldn't want to miss the regional playoffs, even though he wouldn't have the chance to get in the game.

"There's a lot riding on this one," he said.

Lyle looked from his game. "Tell her we'll get off the Interstate if that's what she's worried about. There's a highway that leads into Mueller Road, just behind the hockey rink. It's two exits up."

"How do you know?"

Lyle got the weary expression which said he didn't suffer stupid questions gladly. "I've got the map pulled up on my tablet, Dad. We *are* in the twenty-first century, you know."

"Watch it, genius, okay? Hear that, Mom?" Ed said louder. "We'll let Mr. Gates here get us to the game. If it gets too bad, we'll spend the night in a motel—" A cheer went up from the back seat. "—but I think it will let up by the time we're finished. Anyway, we'll call when we get there."

Ed told her he loved her and rang off, concentrating on the road which was becoming more and more obliterated by the snow. The visibility was so poor he almost missed the exit for Mueller Road. Skidding down the exit ramp, he turned toward the small town where the game was being held and found the road hadn't been cleared recently.

"Wrong move, Mr. Gates. Got another call?"

Without looking, Ed felt Lyle's eyes on him.

"Keep going, Dad. This is the play off for the Regionals and the map says it only fifteen miles to the high school."

"Fifteen miles in this weather is like going through a field full of cotton candy. It'll take twice, maybe three times, as long."

"We're not scheduled to play the first game anyway." Lyle was his team's best goalie and Ed knew if the relief goalie had to fill in, the team would lose. But he couldn't just park and sit in the car until the next snow plow came by.

Miraculously, the snow treads dug in and found traction. The SUV moved faster, up to thirty mph and, again, the boys in the back cheered. They had just cleared a slight rise when the headlights picked up something moving across the road.

A deer took a few steps and stood directly in their path. Its eyes glowing through the snow, the buck stared at the oncoming vehicle. Ed only had time to yell, "Hold on, boys!" before the SUV skidded to a stop. Then the deer took its time about moving on, as though it were reminding the humans that it owned the road and surrounding fields.

"That was close. Everybody okay? You know what they say, where there's one deer, three are nearby, so be on the lookout."

"Yeah, Dad, let's get to the game." They had only gone a half a mile when they saw the skid marks going off the road and disappearing into the trees. Although they were rapidly being covered with snow, Lyle spotted them as he was looking for more deer. "Dad, I think a car must have gone off the road."

"We better take a look, then. Won't be many crazy people out tonight beside us." Ed and the boys pulled over and, leaving their emergency lights blinking and taking a flashlight, followed the tracks until they came to a fence with a large portion torn down. "Looks bad. You boys better stay here."

Though he could barely make out the wreck, so covered with snow that it looked more like an uprooted tree than a vehicle, Ed could see oil dripping, forming a black puddle in the snow. Dreading what he would find, he shone the flashlight into the wreck. Surely no one could have survived hitting a tree and turning over. He could make out that it was the wreck of an older-model car, probably without air bags. Confirming his worst fears, there was a body wedged between the steering wheel and the driver's seat, covered with blood. The doors were jammed from the impact.

"Lyle," he shouted.

"Right here, Dad," said a calm voice right behind him.

"Call nine-one-one. Tell them where we are and—"

"I already have. They said they'd get here as soon as they could. The dispatcher said they're very busy clearing other accidents. I'll get the blankets and first aid kit out of the car. Anything else?"

"And the fire extinguisher. I don't like that oil leak under the car—"

That's when they heard the first wail from the backseat. Ed shone the flashlight in direction of the sound and saw a car seat strapped to the tilted backseat with a baby in it.

"Holy—" Remembering Lyle was within hearing distance, Ed amended his language. "—cow! It's a baby!"

"It's not like you haven't seen one before. It must be cold. No telling how long it's been there."

"No, wait!"

Before his father could stop him, Lyle had climbed through the broken window of the wrecked car, and retrieved the infant, handing him out to Ed. He was climbing out of the wreck, when the car shifted and smoke started pouring out of the smashed engine.

"Jump, Lyle!"

"But what about the lady, Dad? She's badly hurt!"

Lyle climbed over the front seat and unbuckled the woman's seat belt. With his arms under hers, he eased her out of the driver's seat and over to Ed who dragged her through the window and onto the snow. She moaned as Michael came running with the fire extinguisher. The other two boys were right behind him with the blanket and first aid kit.

When the paramedics and the police arrived, they found the baby and the woman wrapped in blankets lying on the tailgate of the SUV. Ed was using the last quarter tank of gas keeping car warm and the boys were taking turns entertaining the baby.

As the paramedics were transferring the woman to the ambulance, Lyle caught Ed's arm. "Look, Dad, it's the deer."

The buck was standing at the edge of the tree line, watching them with glowing eyes that shone through the snow like beacons in a storm. Covered with snow, it appeared to be pure white except for its eyes and antlers.

"Now that's a tempting shot," said one of the policemen behind them. "That's a four point buck. The wife wants a rack like that for over the fireplace at home."

As if the deer had heard him, he turned and vanished among the trees.

Ed's wife called back to say that Lyle's game had been cancelled, and they'd all better stay in a motel for the night. She'd call Lyle's teammates' parents and let them know.

Ed didn't get much sleep that night because he was sharing a room with four boys and because he kept worrying about the woman and the baby. He looked over at Lyle who was stretched beside him. He wasn't asleep either.

"Did I tell you how proud I was of you tonight? Sorry about the game, though."

Lyle shrugged. "No big deal. There'll be other games."

"I was thinking about whether they'll survive that awful crash, the woman especially. The baby will be okay, the paramedics said."

"I was thinking about the deer. If it hadn't stopped us when it did, we would have gone right by the wreck, wouldn't we? We only slowed down because we were looking for more deer."

"And because the plow hadn't been there yet. Yeah, I guess you could say that. Yeah. Don't tell me you're worried it's going to end up on somebody's plate as chili. Deer cause so many accidents, here in Iowa, they call them cows with antlers."

Lyle looked over at his father. "I think it was trying to warn us, Dad."

"Like holding up a 'Go Slow' sign, wreck up ahead? Come on." Ed punched Lyle's arm. "Ow! That's a real goalie's biceps!"

But Lyle's mind was somewhere else. "The Plains Indians have a legend about shape shifters—spirit animals, they call them. They can either do harm or good, depending on who they show themselves to. If they show themselves to a bad guy, that means harm. If they show themselves to a good person that means something good's going to happen."

"I don't know, kid. Your game was the last one of the season. After this, the hockey rink becomes the baseball field. And I wouldn't call that poor woman's wreck very lucky. Hope she has insurance."

Lyle heaved a sigh and closed his laptop. "Good night, Dad. You know what?"

"What's that, Mr. Gates?"

"You're a good person, but a little bit dense."

The next morning, they were having breakfast in the motel with the TV news blaring over the guests as they ate their choice of cereal. The announcer was chronicling all the events of the previous night. He ended with "Here's a story to warm your heart. At five, a young single mother finished up her job as a waitress at a highway truck stop and picked up her eighteen month old son from the sitter. Then she started home just as the blizzard struck. She never made it."

He went on to say that the woman who lived alone, skidded off the country road and hit a tree. The car overturned, leaving the mother badly hurt and the baby in the backseat.

"They lay there while cars kept passing on the road, but no one noticed the wreck lying in the woods until two and a half hours later when a car came along full of boys going to a hockey game."

"Hey, that's us!" the boys yelled.

Chapter 13

VIOLETTE

The place had been there as long as anyone living could remember, a monument to what some considered the pinnacle of success, and others considered the epitome of excess. Belle Reve, French for beautiful dream, still stood among its gardens, looking like an old beauty at a debutante's ball.

When Casey was growing up, her aunt's comfortable split-level was just down the tree-lined street from Belle Reve. She and the neighborhood kids used to play there in its lush gardens, despite the city's surly head gardener running them off every time he caught them, threatening to call the police if he caught them again. The house was unoccupied, only open at Christmas and for garden tours in the spring when the azaleas burst out like fireworks.

The vast grounds of the ante-bellum mansion made it perfect for games of Hide-and-Seek and Kick-the-Can and, of course, War. It was during one of those games they discovered the *garconniere*, a sort of French version of the garage apartment where the young men of the family could sow their wild oats without disturbing their prominent parents—or their reputation. The two-story round building was hidden by a wall of gardenia bushes, its jalousied shutters closed to prying eyes.

Of course, the place was haunted. Like every other antebellum mansion, this one had its ghosts. The neighborhood gang rehearsed them like a catechism to entertain the busloads of tourists who came to see the gardens. There was a rumor that things flew through the air, and strange wailings came from the house during the night. Another pundit said there was an old Indian curse on the house, that it was built over an Indian graveyard. Then there was the Lady in the White Dress who appeared in an upstairs window once a year in the month of June.

Casey's Aunt Antonia was an unbeliever, though. With snapping black eyes, Tony defied any ghost to lower her property values. "Hogwash! I live right next door to the place, and I would know if there was anything living or dead in there. And believe you me, they're all dead a long time ago."

One day, somebody broke the lock on the *garconniere*—the big chicken coop somebody called it— and they went in, boys first. Mice scurried, bats and even birds flew out of the upper story as the mighty moved up the winding stairs followed by the cautious. On the second floor, they found a jumble of furniture—bed frames with mattresses which spawned generations of mice, tables and chairs stacked on top, and what looked like a flea market on top of that. The odor of gardenias lay on the dead air like flowers on a grave.

"Looks like my room," one of the boys remarked.

The children all gave dusty laughs. The more adventurous went on to the top discovering two more bedrooms as they went.

"Must've had one helluva sleepover back in the day," somebody said.

Casey didn't want her aunt to see her on the balcony at the top so she stayed on the second floor, poking around. Among the clutter on the beds, she found a small book. It was covered with dust, brown, and stiff with age. She guiltily slipped it into her jeans pocket, looking over her shoulder as she did so. It wasn't stealing, she told herself. It was just a loan. She would put it back the next time she came over. On the way downstairs, her hand brushed an indentation on the wall. It was dark, the summer sun barely lit the stairs, and only a little of the wall. She traced it with her fingers. Her eyes adjusted to the faint light and she saw what her fingers confirmed.

Someone had carved a heart with the initials *S R loves V T* in it.

Sitting on the steps of the big house, she thumbed through the pages of the book, discovering that it was poetry, written in flowery words she couldn't begin to pronounce, let alone understand. But there in the fly leaf, she saw an inscription in a style of handwriting matching the elaborate words inside. *To my dear Sebastian with undying love, Your Violette. PS: Remember me.* Sebastian to match the S and Violette to match the V. So Sebastian R. loves Violette T.

It was nearly twenty years before Casey came back to the house. By that time she had a daughter of her own now, and the new occupants, a doctor and his wife, had invited her daughter Sarah to play with their five-year-old Holly. Feeling guilty, Casey rehearsed what she was going to say when she returned to perfect strangers a book she had "borrowed" years before.

But her gracious hostess, Sasha, just laughed when Casey tried to give her the book she had taken from the *garconniere* years before. "Oh, keep it, please! You don't know how many truckloads of stuff we had to haul out of that old place before we tore it down. Tons and tons! So you did us a big favor by taking it, honestly."

Sasha gave her a brief tour around the house while doing a standup routine on the perils of renovating old houses. "Who needs a gym when you've got two flights of stairs to climb just to get to the bathroom?"

"You're lucky it wasn't outside," Casey answered, keeping a lookout for mice. She had a childhood memory of droves of them scurrying out of her way.

"Oh, is that what it was? We wondered what that was. Anyway the builders tore it down."

When they finally sat down to minted iced tea, Casey told her about playing on the grounds as a child and how she had come to discover the book in the *garconniere*. "I'm afraid we were a bunch of hooligans, always dodging Mr. Lynch, the gardener hired by the city to look after the place. He used to shout at us and threaten to flatten us with his shovel if he ever got close enough. Lucky for us, he never did."

" Probably didn't want anybody horning in on his racket. I think he was the one they said stole all the garden statues and urns." Sasha giggled nervously and suddenly stiffened as though listening for something. "Did anybody ever say anything about this house being haunted? You know, ghosts?"

"You've been listening to the local gossips. They say that about every old house around here." Casey didn't feel perfectly honest, not leveling with Sasha about the specific rumors circulating about Belle Reve. But then, Casey hadn't seen anything that would make her believe otherwise. They were just old tales.

"Really?" Sasha looked relieved. "You're so refreshing! You have no idea how good that is to hear."

"Just talk to my Aunt Tony. She'll set you straight.

She's not a believer in gossip or ghosts. Why, what makes you think there's anything to the stories?"

"Oh, I don't know. I feel silly even talking about it."

"Not as silly as I felt returning a book I'd taken eighteen years before." She told Sasha about the carving she had seen on the stairwell of the *garconniere* and how it matched the names on the inscription in the book of poetry. "Here, I'll show you." She opened the stiff cover of the little book and showed her hostess the inscription.

"'To My Dear Sebastian With My Undying Love. Your Violette.'" Sasha looked at Casey. "Any idea who this Sebastian was? And who this girl was that was so crazy about him?"

Casey shook her head. "I thought you might be able to shed some light on that mystery."

"Seriously, not a clue. But I'll tell something. I don't believe in ghosts, but there's something going on here. For one thing, I can't get anybody to help me in the house. I've called the agency and the girls work here for a week and just when I think they're going to stay, they quit." Sasha snapped her fingers. "Like that!"

"My aunt says those are mostly college girls the agency hires. I'll ask her to find somebody local."

Just then the two little girls raced out on the porch. "Mommy, Mommy, we just saw the lady again." Holly climbed up in her mother's lap. "She came in the door of the bedroom and went straight through the wall!"

"And the vase on the mantel changed places. I saw it with my eyes!" Sarah looked as if she enjoying herself. "It was cool!"

"Maybe it was our girl Violette." Sasha cuddled her daughter closer. "Don't worry, Mommy will have a talk with her, she can't scare you like that." Looking at Casey, she said, "See what I mean? We've added a ghost to our family."

Casey left, still holding the book she now felt held clues to whoever Violette was. As soon as Sarah went down for a nap after lunch, Casey got on the internet and looked up the state website of historical places. There was Belle Reve in all its Greek Revival splendor, built in 1840, twenty years before the Civil War. Its builder was one Seagrove Raynor, a wealthy lawyer, businessman, and state representative in the legislature. Unfortunately, it only remained in his possession for a short time. After his only son, Sebastian, was killed at Petersburg, Raynor sold the house and moved to Texas where he died. The house was sold several times afterward, finally becoming a girls' school, and then an apartment building.

So Sebastian R. was Sebastian Raynor, killed in the Civil War. Poor Violette! She was so in love with him. Must have been an awful shock, Casey thought. She then looked up Seagrove Raynor. There were three whole paragraphs on that illustrious man with a string of references, many of the titles of books and articles referring to the removal of the Southeastern Native

Americans. Apparently, Raynor had made his money swindling the natives out of their land. Moreover, having been a state legislator and friend of the governor, Raynor had been instrumental in convincing the legislators to declare the Indians hostile to the settlers, and therefore, removed west.

With the proceeds from the land swindle, Raynor had built Belle Reve which slowly became his nightmare as the Civil War ground the South under Sherman's iron wheels of vengeance. His only son's coffin, while being shipped home, was lost when the ship went down in a sudden storm.

But as much as she had learned about the origins of Belle Reve, Casey still found nothing about Violette. It certainly wasn't Raynor's wife whose name was Belinda. Young Sebastian wasn't married when he died at Petersburg so who was Violette T?

"Well, why didn't you ask me? I could have told you that!" Aunt Antonia was still an aging rose, but everyone noticed the thorns had grown sharper as she approached ninety. "All this time you thought you were keeping a secret from me, but I know you, missy. I know that guilty look on your face when you've done something wrong. Not that taking anything from that old place would have been wrong. You should have seen the antiques that new couple put out on the curb for the city to haul away. The dealers were on it like turkey vultures on road kill."

Antonia digressed from antique dealers to prices for chandeliers to the walnut tea cart she lost years ago at a yard sale for charity. "Somebody sold it right out from under the cookies and lemonade."

"Aunt Tony, you were saying you knew who this Violette was," Casey prodded gently.

"So I was, so I was. I'm trying to think of the story my grandmother told me about that family. Her mother used to play next door as a little girl just like you did. That was when it used to belong to Colonel Edwards, of course. That house has changed hands more times than a two dollar bill, you know."

Afraid her aunt would ramble down the list of owners, Casey said again," And what was the story, Tony?"

"Don't rush me, dear. Some scandal about a mistress, I remember. Wife went off like a shot back to her relatives in Savannah. More tea? And I think Ida made some fresh oatmeal cookies this morning."

Before Casey could stop her, her aunt called Ida from the kitchen. Ida was almost as old as her employer and nearly as grumpy. She had been with Casey's aunt through three marriages, several scandals, and a horde of nieces and nephews. She stood in the doorway, one wary eye on Sarah, playing in the living room, and the other on the level of tea in the pitcher.

"Don't drink so much tea, Miss Tony. You know you can't hold it 'til you gets to the bathroom."

"Thank you, Ida. I don't need you to go around broadcasting it. Bring some of those oatmeal cookies you made—"

"Now, you know what the doctor said about you limiting your sweets, Miz Tony."

Finally Casey interrupted the squabble looming over Tony's sugar intake for the last twenty-four hours. "Do you remember who Violette was, Ida? You know, the house next door—"

"You mean the ghost of that girl that still haunts the upstairs in that old place? I sure do. That's why nobody will work there, that and those stairs. That house was built back in the day when they had upstairs folks and folks for downstairs like on TV." Ida settled into a chair with a groan and took up her story. "My granny said, back in the day, some of her relatives worked in that house. Said some old Indians put a curse on the place that was built on the blood of their people. They said that the man who built that fine house didn't even pay them the few bucks he promised for their land. When some of them came and tried to collect from him, he run them off."

"But who was Violette?" Casey tried to keep the impatience out of her voice but Ida seemed as prone to digression as her aunt.

But unlike her aunt, Ida wouldn't be prodded. "Hold on, I'm getting round to that, missy. So when the son grows up, he goes off to college in Virginia."

"Oh, that's right!" Antonia's face lit up with the memory. "Didn't he get some girl pregnant who worked in a whorehouse?" Seeing Casey's disapproving expression, she added, "That was all that was over there across the river at the time. Houses of ill repute and stills. Lots of stills. Whiskey and wild, wild women!"

Ida was shaking her head, making a tsk-tsk noise with her tongue. "See there, that's how rumors get started." Ida crossed her arms, with a scowl on her face that would stop a clock. "You don't know the truth, Miz Tony, so just hush and let me tell it, hear?" Antonia sucked in her breath, but she knew better that to cross Ida, so she gave up. "She wasn't no hoochie-mama, so that's just wrong," Ida stated. "Her mama was Creole from New Orleans, mistress to a fine gentleman, who was part Indian himself. When Violette was born, he claimed her as his own, and raised with a silver spoon. When she was old enough, he sent her to boarding school in South Carolina and that's where she met Raynor's son at some dance or cotillion or other. They fell in love—she was beautiful and he was good-looking. They would have made a perfect couple 'cept for one thing. They had the same father."

Both Casey's and Antonio's mouths fell open as they gasped collectively. Ida looked satisfied at the impact her revelation had made. "That's right! Old Raynor was the father of Violette, amongst a lot of others. That old dog had lots of women on the side, Indian, white, black.

Could have populated a whole county back then." Ida went off hee, hee, heeing, shoulders shaking, fanning herself with one hand.

Antonia sniffed. "I don't think it was that funny. Those poor kids. Men are such dogs."

"But if they both had the same last name, wasn't that a clue that they were related? " Casey could imagine the scene at the dance, handsome Sebastian bowing to Violette. Raynor meeting Raynor. "I mean, wouldn't that be a clue?"

Ida wiped her eyes with her long, brown fingers. "Well, that's what fooled everybody. See, Big Daddy gave her everything but his name. Violette had her mama's last name, Toussaint or something French like that. So neither one of them knew until Big Daddy dropped the lead balloon on them."

"Then what happened? They never got married, I take it." Casey was silently thankful for DNA testing. "Because Sebastian died in the Civil War."

"Oh, honey, it all went down 'way before that." Ida leaned forward in her chair. "Big Daddy found out the lovers were planning to elope and spilled the beans about both of them being his kids. That's when Sebastian joined the Militia and Violette hung herself. Story goes she got one of her friends that worked there to let her into the house while the master and his wife were away at church, They came home and there she was, hanging from the chandelier in Sebastian's upstairs bedroom. They say that her ghost still haunts that same room. Some folks've seen her in the window of that room, looking out to see if they're coming home from church."

"Or if Sebastian is coming home from the war. How sad." Casey was wondering if she should tell Sasha this story or just let it fade into history where it had been buried until she had taken the book from the *garconniere*.

"We saw her, Holly and me." Sarah had come in while they were wrapped up in Ida's story. "She came in that bedroom door and went through the wall just like that. And a vase over the fireplace changed places. Honest!" The child looked at their faces and nodded. "Honest," she said again.

"Maybe she brought some flowers with her," Ida said. "And was deciding where to put them."

Sarah nodded as if that explained a vase taking off of its own accord. "I think they were gardenias. We smelled gardenias."

Casey had a sudden memory of the day she had found the book Violette had given Sebastian. The air was heavy with the smell of gardenias and she remembered there was a bower of gardenias outside the broken window of the *garconniere*.

Next time, Sasha asked her to come over, Casey asked to see the upstairs bedrooms again, making up an excuse of wanting to see the color of paint Sasha had used on the walls. She went into the upstairs bedroom that looked out on the road, the one where Sarah had seen the vase change places. Sure enough, the vase was there on the fireplace mantle, a porcelain vase sprinkled with hand-painted flowers. Case looked closer. The little flowers were violets. She picked it up and looked at the bottom. It was signed VT.

"You can have that old thing, if you want it," Sasha's voice said from behind her. "I keep meaning to throw it away but forgetting about it with everything else I've got to do."

"Oh, I think it belongs in here, don't you? I mean, it goes with the soft lavender color on the walls."

Sasha sighed. "I guess so. Anyway, it's the guest room so it really not a priority, is it?"

"Definitely not." Casey followed her hostess out of the room, silently whispering a fond goodbye.

Chapter 14

THE BOY WHO THOUGHT HE WAS A HORSE

Before penicillin, which was the first true antibiotic, doctors had difficulty controlling infections, especially cases of virulent fevers and sepsis. The manufacture of penicillin was only in the trial stages at the end of World War II and it was only available to the men serving in the armed forces.

When the war ended, the hospitals were filled to the limit with wounded, and there were no beds for civilians, except in life-or-death cases. So when the child came down with a high fever, his family called the hospital and was told, not only that they had no beds, but that there were no doctors available.

"With all the wounded and dying, we certainly don't need a child with an infectious disease in the hospital," the exasperated nurse on the phone said. "Call the Health Department if the child gets worse."

The fever was 102 degrees by the time the nurse arrived. The child was listless and clammy to the touch, except his head was hot. She bathed him in alcohol and cold water, but his temperature only went higher, to nearly 105 degrees.

She gave the family instructions to keep bathing him, but the child kept mumbling and flailing his arms. Finally, he grew quiet and they got some sleep. The fever lasted for four days and the little boy slipped into unconsciousness.

"I'm afraid it's scarlet fever," the nurse said. She was a young woman who had a child of her own.

"Isn't there anything you can do?" The little boy's mother wiped her eyes on her apron. "His father is fighting in the Pacific and hasn't seen him in three years."

The nurse shook her head. As used as she was to people dying, with a child it was different. She thought of her son, what it would mean to lose him. "There's no cure for it, unfortunately. It's the high fever that kills or leaves the patient severely impaired."

She gave them a yellow sign that said *QUARANTINED. DO NOT ENTER* and told no one to enter his room except to bring him food. That person would not be allowed to leave the house either. "And one more thing. All his toys will have to be burned—books, everything."

Meanwhile, the child was having a long dream of riding wild horses through canyons of clouds, gripping their flowing manes with both hands. He galloped and galloped through the towering peaks, through sprays of mist that left him cool and wet.

The nurse telephoned on the fourth night to see how the child was. "No change," the mother said despondently. "He hasn't regained consciousness enough to eat anything. He's not eaten in four days."

"Are you willing to take a chance? I have to know because I'm at the hospital where my friend says he can get me a syringe of penicillin. It's a new medicine that fights infections, but there are rumors it's made from horse serum."

"I don't care if it's made from monkeys. My son is dying. I'll try anything. "

"I'm just warning you it hasn't really been tried on children yet. I'll have to experiment with different dosages."

"Can you bring it tonight?" the frantic mother asked.

"I'll do better than that. I'll make him my first stop on my rounds."

With the first injection, the boy's temperature came down. With the second injection, he opened his eyes. The nurse's cool hand was on his forehead when he looked up and saw her smiling face.

"Hello. You've been gone a long time. Where have you been?"

"Riding horses through the clouds," he said. "Are you an angel?"

When the nurse told the mother what her son had said, she replied, "That's funny. He's always been afraid of horses. But he's right, you are an angel. You've performed a miracle."

"Not me. It was that horse penicillin."

When the boy had recovered, he went in search of horses while his mother was at work. There were none close by because he lived in an apartment in the city. So he read books about them and drew beautiful pictures of all kinds of horses. He felt a kind of kinship with them. He was weak so they would be his strength.

When the war ended and his father came home from the war, he asked his son what he wanted to replace all his toys which had been burned.

"A horse of my own," the child said.

His father smiled. "And just where are you going to keep this horse? In your closet?"

So the boy went in search of a pasture even though he was still weak from his illness. But the only pasture he found already had horses in it, scrubby little cowponies with matted manes and tails. The boy lured them to the pasture fence with grass and then climbed on their backs, riding them until he fell off. Far from being discouraged, he would climb back on again, this time gripping tighter with his weak legs. This way, he found that he could control the pony by exerting pressure with his heels. When he was tired, he spoke to them, telling him about his sickness and riding through the clouds.

His father left his mother for another woman who didn't nag him all the time, and the boy's mother married again, this time to a man who wanted him to play football "like other boys." When he refused, his stepfather beat him. When the boy was fifteen, he ran away and, after two days of wandering, found a stable on the edge of city. The owner discovered him asleep in empty stall, reminding him of himself at that age. Waking the boy up, the owner said he needed a stable hand and offered the boy a job mucking out stalls if he would finish high school. Later, he taught the boy to ride and then to take the horses over jumps. This was a show stable, making tours of the show circuits on both coasts and competing in Europe.

The boy soon earned enough money to buy his own horse that he called Angel. He fell in love with the owner's daughter and had a son of his own. But he never forgot his dream of riding through the canyons of clouds or the nurse who saved his life.

By calling the Public Health Service and giving the year he had contracted scarlet fever, he finally tracked her down. She lived in a home for retired nurses and, when he explained who he was, she remembered him immediately.

"You're the boy who rode wild horses through the clouds," she said, laughing. "I've always remembered what you said. It sounded like so much fun. You have to be careful, though. Riding wild horses can be dangerous."

The week after he visited her, he got on a strange horse. He talked to it, but it didn't answer. It didn't want to cooperate either. He had never had one like that, but he decided to take the strange horse over a few jumps anyway.

On the approach to the second jump, the horse suddenly planted his feet and stopped. His rider hit the wooden bars of the jump in just the wrong way. The last thing he heard was the snap of his neck. The next thing he knew he was back where he most wanted to be, clinging to the mane of a wild horse, riding through the canyon of clouds.

About the Author

Even as a child, Trisha O'Keefe was impressed by the inherent power of alternative medicines. Indigenous healing practices are an ongoing theme in her novels. As a native Southerner, O'Keefe claims to have "a lot of red dirt" flowing in her veins. Growing up, she spent summers on her uncle's farm in South Georgia, "mainly getting into trouble." That trend has continued throughout her life. After traveling abroad for fourteen years, running into revolutions or governmental coups nearly everywhere she went—even Britain was in the midst of a labor strike when she moved there—she returned to the States. She is the daughter of Jimmy Jones, a well-known journalist for the *Atlanta Constitution* under Editor Ralph Magill.

One of her earliest memories was the sound of a typewriter rattling away in the middle of the night. You would think that would have cured her from ever putting two words together, let alone a book. Still, at age 6, she co-wrote *Spot, The Dog* with her sister, followed a long time later by *Hanahatchee, Poseidon's Eye*, and

Lovesong of the Chinaberry Man. Two more novels, *The Magi's Well,* and *The Mama Tree* were published in 2016. "I guess some things you can't cure," O'Keefe says. "You just have to go where they take you."

www.ingramcontent.com/pod-product-compliance
Lightning Source LLC
Chambersburg PA
CBHW070959120726
47910CB00004B/1308